This story is
incidents are
locations, or e

ISBN: 978-1-989206-40-9

To Chris and Charlie

# FOOD FRIGHT

## NICO BELL

# Chapter One

## Cassie Adler

*Virginia, 1995*

Cassie Adler gnawed her thumbnail until she tasted blood. Crickets chirped as a slight breeze cooled the September night air, cutting through the thick Virginia humidity. She shifted on her feet and looked past the dim streetlights lining the parking lot of Rochelle High School. A truck's high beams switched to low as it drew closer.

Her chest tightened.

This was a mistake, but she'd come too far to wimp out now. Heather and her friends would never let Cassie hear the end of it if she didn't follow through with the plan. Besides, this is what she wanted, right?

To be one of them.

Because if she belonged to their group, the teasing would stop.

No more jabs about her loser father.

No more jokes about Cassie's skeleton build or frizzy brown hair.

No more mocking her mom, who spent more nights sleeping in the county jail than her own bed back home.

Cassie just needed to complete this one small task and she'd finally be in their circle, no longer standing on the outside.

A sour taste settled in her mouth as she forced a smile. The truck pulled up to the curb and freshman, Jennifer Shipley stepped out. Even with just a few lights and the sliver of moon gleaming down, her green eyes shined. A sloppy bun sat at the crown of her head and baggy soccer shorts hung low on her hips. The Nike shirt Jennifer wore cost more than Cassie's entire thrift store outfit combined.

"I've never done anything like this before." Jennifer's nervous laugh echoed through the night. "My mom's going to kill me if she finds out I drove on only my permit."

"It's worth the risk." Cassie straightened her back, swallowed the knot in her throat. "Come on. Everyone's waiting."

"This is crazy." A smile settled on Jennifer's thin lips as she followed Cassie to the school's glass doors. "How'd you guys get inside? Doesn't this place have an alarm?"

"Yeah, but Heather stole her mom's key. Again. And she knows how to disarm the security system."

"She stole Coach's key? Impressive." Jennifer stopped in the foyer of the high school. "So, what's going to happen next?"

"It's just a little initiation, like we said at practice. We want to welcome you to the team." They started down the hallway towards the gym. "It's pretty cool that you made varsity as a freshman."

"Thanks. Soccer is really the only thing I'm good at."

Envy tainted Cassie's mouth. "You're lucky. I've been trying to get on the team since my freshman year."

"Really?" She tilted her head. "I saw your bicycle kick at practice. You've got plenty of natural skill."

Warmth spread to Cassie's cheeks. She slowed her pace. "My friend Jamie is tutoring me, trying to get my grades up so I can qualify for an athletic scholarship next year, but that's never going to happen."

"The grades or the scholarship?"

"Both." Cassie shrugged. "Not a big deal really. I mean, not many people leave Rochelle."

Except her dad. Apparently, he couldn't get away fast enough. Cassie shook off the thought.

Jennifer gave Cassie a little nudge. "Hey, you don't know what's going to happen. I mean, I hoped I'd make the soccer team, but I didn't know for sure. And now, here I am."

Cassie nodded. Heather and her crew didn't make the varsity soccer team until their junior years.

9

Now, as seniors, their passions lain not only on the field, but in tormenting underclassmen.

They reached the gym.

Cassie paused, her stomach churning. "You know, if you don't want to do this, I could just say you didn't show."

"No. I want to." Jennifer's eyes widened. "I mean, I appreciate that you're always looking out for me at practice, but I should probably try and make friends with the rest of the team, right? And if this is what it takes, then I'm in."

"Sure. Um, okay. Ready?"

Jennifer nodded and pushed open the doors.

Halogen lights shined down on the waxed gym floor. Heather Wilson, the ringleader of the group, stood in the middle of the gym, a large duffle bag beside her. Her long blonde hair hung past her shoulders, always smooth, not like Cassie's hair that knotted like Christmas lights—and just as hard to untangle.

Heather jutted out her hip and crossed her arms over her chest. "Geez, we've been waiting."

"Yeah, we still need to study for our Bio test." Erin Shifflett tilted her head toward Lauren Fisher, both frowned as they regarded Jennifer.

Unlike Jennifer whose natural beauty shined without make-up, Erin and Lauren painted on their prettiness. And not very well. Even from a few feet away, Cassie spotted the outline of Lauren's foundation along her round jaw.

She cast her eyes back toward Heather. "We can do this another time. I mean, if you guys have to leave soon."

Lauren sighed. "No, we're all here now. Let's just get this over with."

Jennifer's smiled faltered. "So, it's just us? Where's the rest of the team?"

"We're the ones who do the initiating." Heather motioned to Erin and Lauren.

Cassie chewed her fingernail.

"I'm the captain after all, and these are the best players." Heather's eyes narrowed. "Well, until you came along."

Jennifer let out a nervous laugh, her eyes darting from one teammate to the next. She fidgeted with the hem of her t-shirt.

"You think you're so great, don't you?" Lauren stepped up and pushed Jennifer's shoulder.

"What? No. No better than anyone else."

Erin reached into the duffle bag and pulled out a roll of duct tape. "Everyone thinks they're the best at first. Well, except Cassie, but that's only because she's smart enough to know her place."

Cassie's shoulders slumped.

"But it's our job, as team leaders, to teach humility." Heather flicked her head, a quick motion that sent Erin and Lauren into action.

Erin grabbed Jennifer's arms and pinned them back.

"Hey, stop it." Panic laced Jennifer's voice as Erin started to drag her toward the soccer goal, which was set up at the far end of the gym.

"Cassie, get her feet."

But Cassie remained planted, flinching as Jennifer let out another panicked plea.

"Cassie," Heather hissed.

"Okay, fine. I'm coming." She hated the weakness in her voice, the pathetic tone that haunted her memories, that begged her dad not to abandon her, that pleaded with her mom to stop drinking, that resigned her to living with a bitter grandmother. And here it surfaced again, the pitiful melody of a coward.

"I'm sorry. Try not to struggle or it will only last longer." Cassie grabbed Jennifer's feet, they flailed in rebellion and she squeezed tight.

"Hold her steady." Lauren peeled off a strip of tape and started to wrap it around one of Jennifer's hands.

"I thought we were friends." Jennifer's voice rose an octave as she looked to Cassie.

Cassie turned her back as Heather dumped the contents of the bag onto the floor.

Melons thumped and rolled.

"I know we're not supposed to use our hands in soccer, but tonight, we make an exception." Heather picked one up. "Get her ready for target practice."

"No, please." Jennifer twisted.

"I can't tie her to the post if she's squirming." Erin tried to grab her hand again, but Jennifer thrust around. She lost her hold and Jennifer yanked her other hand free. "Shit, grab her."

But Jennifer moved quick. She balled up a fist and punched Erin's gut. Erin winced and crumbled to the floor, folding in on herself with pain. Jennifer scampered to her feet, swung another punch and connected with Lauren's cheek.

Lauren stumbled backwards, eyes wide, face flaming red.

Jennifer gritted her teeth and shot a look at Cassie.

Fear rippled down Cassie's spine. "I'm sorry."

"A little late for that." Jennifer sprinted for the door, leading back to the hallway.

"Shit, stop her. She'll get us all in trouble." Heather took off, Lauren and Erin regaining composure and bolting. Their sneakers pounded the floor as they chased Jennifer.

"Cassie, help us." Heather held the gym door open and Cassie's feet started moving on autopilot. The girls stood in the hallway, jaws tight. "I'll make sure she doesn't leave from the front. Everyone else, split up. Don't let her get out of the school." Heather ran toward the front door.

Erin and Lauren looked at each other, and for the first time that night, Cassie saw panic in their eyes.

"This is really bad." Lauren shook her head. "We should have done my idea."

"Making her eat a pound of brownies is hardly an initiation. Besides, it's too late now." Erin turned toward Cassie. "We do what Heather said. You take the freshman hall. I've got the back of the school. Lauren, you've got the rest."

And then she ran off.

Lauren's eyes moistened with tears, but she hurried off in the opposite direction leaving Cassie to search the freshman hall.

Lockers lined the walls, punctuated by a classroom doors. She tried a few, but they were locked. Cassie hurried to the end of the hall, an intersection where she could see the front door.

Heather stood like a tiger ready to strike. She spotted Cassie. "She hasn't come through. Truck is still on the curb."

"How do we know she didn't just bolt and leave the truck?"

Heather's eyes widened, a slice of fear cutting into her sharp features. "Where would she have gone?"

True. Dense trees lined the property and mountains sat on the edge of the horizon. Part of the many qualities of living in Rochelle, a rural town in the middle of nowhere Virginia.

"She's here." But Heather's voice trembled, betraying her confident stance.

Cassie turned and headed back down the hall. She took a deep breath, but her heart raced as she jiggled more locked classroom handles.

Then, she spotted a light. Soft and shining from under the Home Ec room's door. It had to be Jennifer.

Cassie stopped.

Erin turned a corner and halted, Lauren skidding to a stop on her heels behind. "You find her?"

"I don't know." What was she doing? Was all of this worth it?

Erin frowned and looked at the light under the door.

"We can leave. I mean, nothing really happened, right?" Cassie looked to Lauren and back at Erin, whose eyebrows pinched together.

"No, we need to make sure she won't rat us out. You two wait and I'll get Heather. We'll check together." Erin ran down the hall.

"Heather said Jennifer made out with Braden." Lauren looked down at the floor while she spoke. "That's why she wanted to do all this."

"Really?" Cassie's eyes widened—Braden as in Heather's boyfriend. "That doesn't sound like something Jennifer would do."

Lauren shrugged. "How would you know? She's only been in school for a month."

"I don't know. She just seems like a nice person."

"Well, even nice people do stupid things."

Heather appeared with Erin. "Is she in there?"

But before they could reach the door, a scream penetrated through the wall, echoed down the deserted hallway, and sent goosebumps along Cassie's skin.

Lauren's eyes widened. "What was that?"

Another piercing cry soaked through Cassie's heart and rattled her nerves. She shoved Erin out of the way and swung open the Home Ec door. The demonstration table sat in the front of the room, rows of ovens and sinks lined the walls.

Not a soul in sight, but a foul odor filled the air and singed Cassie's nostrils.

Another scream, followed by thumping.

Cassie dropped to her knees and peered into the oven closest to the door.

She gasped.

Jennifer kneeled inside, slamming her palms against the glass. Tears streaked her cheeks as her pale skin flamed a dark shade of pink. The wire coils of the oven blazed red against her bare knees, and

16

bile rose to Cassie's throat when she realized the scent filling the room was burning flesh.

"Help me get her out!" Cassie pulled the handle, but it wouldn't budge. The old ovens didn't always work properly, Cassie knew from her experience in Home Ec. She tugged again as Jennifer wailed.

Lauren grabbed hold too, but the door refused to unlatch.

"Turn it off," Erin's voice came from behind.

Cassie reached for the dials, turned them to the off position, but nothing happened. The coils blazed and a fire sparked beneath Jennifer. Snot and tears dripped from her face as the flames licked her body and curled up her chest, dancing through her hair and scorching it to the roots.

Erin and Heather remained fixed, terror written on their faces as Cassie tried to find the oven's plug. But the unit was built into the cabinet and she couldn't reach behind. She looked around and grabbed a chair. As she hurled it towards the oven's glass door, one final cry came from inside.

And then whimpers as the chair thumped harmlessly against the oven.

Lauren pulled on the handle, tears now rolling down her face, knuckles white.

"Stop!" Heather's voice cracked. "She's dead. Look."

"No, it can't be." Lauren kept tugging, but the

other girls crouched.

The fire died down, the metal coils dimmed back to grey, and Jennifer's charred body remained pressed against the door. Black and crisp, with tufts of smoke still billowing from her skull.

"We need to go." Heather took a step back, eyes wide, voice shaking. "Guys, we have to get out of here right now."

"We can't leave her." Cassie hurried to the small office just off the side of the room where Mrs. Bowers, the Home Ec teacher, worked. "I'm calling the cops." But when she tried to turn the office's doorknob, it jammed.

"No, no, no."

The lights flickered.

Erin yelped.

"We're leaving, right now." Heather grabbed Lauren, who sobbed into her palms, and pulled. Erin followed.

"Guys, we can't just run away. We need to do something."

But they were already gone.

Cassie ran back to the oven, dropped to her knees. She stared at Jennifer, crisp around the edges with bits of oozing flesh falling from her face. "I'm sorry. I'm so sorry."

The lights flickered again.

From behind, she heard a creak, the sound of a

door slowly opening. Her pulse quickened as she turned and looked over her shoulder. The office door opened, just a little.

*Ding.*

The sound of the oven's timer caused her to jump.

Her heart thumped madly as she ran out the door and down the hall, her feet pounding until she reached the front escape. She bolted outside and into the parking lot where the other girls collapsed to the ground. Lauren sobbed. Erin and Heather mirrored each other's shock.

"Guys, we're in deep shit." Cassie turned to eye the school, an eerie feeling tingling down her neck. "Someone saw us."

# Chapter Two

## Emily Bower

Emily Bower leaned against the Home Ec counter and bit back tears.

Another failure.

"Maybe you added the ingredients in reverse order." Audrey Landry, her friend and the high school's art teacher, looked over the scribbles of the spell's ingredients. "Witchcraft is tricky when you're first getting started. You have to be meticulous."

The sunken soufflé sat on the counter, oozing black frothy foam.

"Well, look on the bright side. The spell you infused is supposed to stimulate unrest. I think we can safely say this would at least spark a nasty case of indigestion."

Emily frowned.

"You'll figure it out."

"But time's running out." She shook her head. If she didn't prove her skills before the full moon, the High Priestess wouldn't accept her into the coven.

"We've all been where you are right now, and we've all pushed through. You will too." Audrey gave Emily a light pat on the shoulder.

"I don't get it. I'm such a good baker, so why can't I get these spells right?"

"It's completely different. Look, the full moon doesn't appear until the end of the month. Homecoming night, actually. So, there's time to keep practicing. We'll try again tomorrow, okay?"

Emily's shoulders slumped. "Sure. Thanks for the help."

"Don't forget to cleanse the workspace or else the magic sticks around." Audrey waved and left the classroom.

The wall clock ticked away the evening as Emily flipped through her notes. Did she stir when she was supposed to let it sit? Was the oven set to the right temperature?

A familiar sinking sensation settled in her gut as she sighed, picked up the soufflé, and dropped it into the trash. She gathered the bag, tied it shut, and headed outside to the dumpster.

The night air still held onto its warmth, despite the thumbnail sliver of moon peeking through thick clouds. It never seemed to cool during central Virginia summers. Sweat beaded her upper lip as she tossed the bag and took a moment to roll her shoulders. Her car sat in the faculty parking lot, peaking out around the school's back corner, beckoning her to drive home, curl up on the couch with a TV dinner, and get some rest.

Same thing she did every night.

But by this time next month, she'd be part of a one of the oldest and most revered covens in Virginia, a sisterhood. Instead of nights alone in an empty house, she'd have a family to hang out with. Well, hopefully.

Emily headed back inside. As she swung open the school's side door, the tail end of an echo drifted past.

Her body stiffened. She held her breath and waited.

Nothing but silence.

She let out a long breath, steadied her nerves

and hurried back to her classroom. As she gathered notes from her office, footfalls pounded and the sound caused Emily to jump. She turned and spotted a freshman from her fifth period. Janice? No, Jennifer. Jennifer Shipley. The girl didn't pause. She closed the door behind herself, opened the oven, crawled inside and shut it before Emily managed a peep.

What the hell?

Emily took a step into the room, her eyes focused on the trembling teenager balled up in the oven. Jennifer's eyes looked toward the door before scanning over to Emily. The young girl's chest rose and fell in quick repetition as relief settled the wrinkles creasing her forehead.

"For goodness sakes, get out of there." Emily took another step closer as the girl flattened her hands against the glass and pushed.

The door remained closed.

Jennifer's eyes widened.

"Don't worry." But as Emily said the words, fright crept from the back of her mind. The magic hadn't been cleansed.

Shit, she needed to release the spell before it manifested into something she couldn't control. Emily turned and hurried back into the office.

Jennifer screamed.

"I'm working on it." Emily shuffled through her

notes, cursing with each flip of the page.

Another scream, this time deeper.

The classroom door flung open and one of her first period students, Cassie Adler, hurried inside.

Panic zigzagged through her brain as Emily kept hidden in the office, peaking out just as her former student, Lauren Fisher, raced into the classroom.

Shit. She closed the door with a soft click of the lock and hurried back to her notes. The words blurred together as panicked tears filled her eyes. The girls shouted. More voices she didn't recognize, more fear and confusion. Emily gritted her teeth and slammed her hands over her ears, but the cries seeped through.

And then everything stopped.

The sounds quieted. Tears dripped down her cheeks as she stepped with trembling knees. She laid her hand on the door, leaned her body close, and pressed her ear to the wood.

"I'm calling the cops."

The doorknob jiggled.

Emily bit her lower lip as she stumbled backwards, staring at the lock, knowing it'd keep the girls out, but feeling no safety. What if they really called the police? Could she escape before they came? What if they find her, cowering in the office? How would she explain herself?

What would the High Priestess do to her when

23

she discovered that magic caused this?

More talking came from the other side of the door and then the lights flickered.

The door unlocked.

Emily covered her open mouth with her hand, biting back a scream as the door slowly crept open.

Feet pounded the floor and the sound faded away.

She fought against the growing dread rising in her gut and managed to step over the threshold. The air hung heavy, a rancid smell drifting free. Her hands trembled with each step until she stood directly in front of the oven.

Emily clenched her fists until her nails dug into her palms.

*Just do it. You have to look inside.*

Or did she? A quick image ran through her mind, one of her racing to her car, driving to an ATM, emptying her near empty bank account, and hitting the road. It's not like anyone would miss her.

No, she shook her head. She spent most of her life running. First, from her father. Later, from her manipulative girlfriend. Now, she had a home and the first glimpse of a real family.

No, she'd clean up this mess.

Emily breathed in shallow, quick breaths as she squeezed her eyelids shut and lowered herself.

*On the count of three. One, two...*

She opened her eyes and swallowed a scream. Jennifer looked back, one of her eyes melted from the socket, oozing a slimy snail trail down her cheek. Emily swallowed the burning bile rising from her stomach as she started organizing her next movements. The body needed to be disposed of. The entire place wiped clean. It'd take time, all night.

*Okay, I can do it. One thing at a time until it's done.*

She pushed the panic aside, regrouped her nerves and began to work.

By morning, the nightmare would be over.

# Chapter Three

## Cassie Adler

Cassie paced the carpet of Heather's bedroom.

Heather tossed a six-pack of Coors on the bed. "We need this more than my parents." She took one and passed the others around.

"Did you actually see anyone?" Erin flicked open the can's tab, her dark eyes searching Cassie's face. "I mean, did you see a foot or a hand? Anything other than an open door?"

"No, but I could have sworn it was locked and then all of a sudden, it wasn't." Cassie waved away the beer.

"Take it. It'll help." Heather shoved it into Cassie's hand.

She never drank, not after watching how alcohol messed up her mom. She set the beer on the dresser. "The longer we wait, the more trouble we're in. We need to call the cops."

"And say what?" Heather sat on her bed, opening a can and taking a gulp.

"The truth. We killed her." Lauren sat on the floor, her back against the wall. Her face paled and a distant expression shadowed her delicate features.

"That's not what happened." Erin sat next to Heather. "Look, if there was someone else in the room, maybe that's who turned on the oven."

"No." Heather snapped. "We basically ran through the halls screaming our lungs off. If any teachers were working late, they'd have come out and stopped us. No one was there. Cassie, you probably thought the door was locked, but it was just jammed or something."

"But—,"

"No one was there. No teachers, no psycho murderers looking to stuff a freshman soccer player in an oven."

Erin sighed. "You're right. We did check ahead of time. The place was empty. I'm positive."

"What if someone came to the school late? In between the time you checked and the time Jennifer

26

ran through the halls?"

"Cassie, let it go." The threat hung in the air as Heather's eyes narrowed.

"It was our fault." Lauren looked up at Cassie. "She trusted you. I saw how you and her talked during practice. I know that you two got along. That's why we asked you to bring her, because we knew she'd do it if her only friend asked."

Cassie's bottom lip trembled. Her throat tightened as tears clouded her eyes and then ran down her cheeks. What had she done? What had she let Heather talk her into? "You're right. I got her there, but we all chased her, and the oven must have somehow flicked on when she got in. Maybe she bumped it, I don't know. It doesn't really matter at this point because it won't change anything. She's dead and someone is going to be blamed, which is only more reason for us to go to the cops before they come to us. It'll look worse if we wait."

Heather leaned forward. "No." She held her hand up, palm out as Cassie's mouth opened. "Let's say we do. We tell them exactly what happened, word-for-word. Then what? Best case, it's chalked up to an accident and we're not legally responsible. So what? My mom would kick us all off the team for acting like idiots and our chances of soccer scholarships vanish."

Erin's shoulders slouched. Lauren looked down

at her hands.

"I'm guessing we all want to get out of this stupid small town, yeah? Well, you may have another year to get your grades up," she pointed to Cassie, "but we're seniors. We're going to be filling out college applications soon. None of us can afford to mess things up now."

Cassie sank to the floor, leaned against the dresser. Bile scratched the back of her throat, but she swallowed it down.

Heather's eyes narrowed. "And that's just best case scenario. Worst case, we're found guilty of her death. Or at least, we're somehow legally responsible."

"Because we are." Lauren's whisper barely made it to Cassie's ears.

"We'll go to jail." Erin's grip tightened on her beer.

"Exactly. Maybe if we're lucky, it'll only be probation. Community service. But actual jail time could be up for grabs." Heather leaned forward. "No one knows we were there, and that's how it's going to stay."

"Until they find fingerprints." Cassie let the words slip past her lips without thinking.

"What did you say?" Heather snapped.

"You heard me." A tiny spark of defiance burned in Cassie's gut. "Haven't you seen a single mystery

28

movie? This isn't going to get swept under the rug, and if you think we can just go back to our happy little lives after tonight than you're a stupid—"

"Enough!" Erin looked to Cassie and then Heather, whose eyes had doubled in size. "You really think they're gonna sweep for prints at a freakin' school? There must be hundreds of people who have touched that oven."

Cassie ran a hand down her face, her insides coiled. "So, what's your plan? Just go to school tomorrow like nothing happened? Wait for someone to open the oven and find her?"

"Exactly." Heather sat a little taller, whipped her long hair behind her shoulder. "Let someone else deal with it. If we're lucky, they'll think Jennifer did it on purpose and we'll be in the clear. We get up tomorrow, go to school like it's a normal day, and let things happen naturally."

"Suicide." Erin perked up. "That could work, right?"

"Suicide." The word burned the back of Cassie's throat. "No. Besides, how would she have gotten into the school? And why do it at school? Why not just kill herself at home?"

"Maybe one of the teachers forgot to lock it. Maybe she wanted to make a statement. I don't fucking know, but it won't be our problem." Heather looked at Cassie, a pleading in her blue eyes. "We weren't there tonight, do you understand?"

"Agreed." Erin took a gulp of her beer.

Exhaustion weighed on Cassie, her muscles weak. She side-eyed Lauren on the floor, a ball of her former self, rocking slightly with her knees to her chest.

It wouldn't work. The whole idea was ludicrous, but maybe that was okay.

They deserved to be caught.

Cassie chewed her lip.

"Lauren?" Erin looked to her friend. "Say it out loud."

"We were never there." She murmured the words.

"Cassie?" Erin searched Cassie's eyes.

"Whatever. It's not like my opinion really counts."

"Don't be like that." Erin sighed. "We need to know you're with us."

But a nagging sensation tugged at her gut. It wasn't just the guilt racing through her nerves, but the unsettled feeling of seeing the door open.

Could it have just been jammed? It wasn't unfathomable. It's not like she saw anyone, or heard footsteps.

"You've been through so much already." Heather slid off the bed and rested her hand on Cassie's knee. "Your dad leaving, and then everything that happened with your mom."

Cassie's jaw twitched. "I'm tired of you talking about my family." There was a slight growl beneath the words, the sudden bit of courage shocking Heather who took back her hand. "Ever since I joined the team, you always bring up my parents. I'm sick of it."

Heather's eyes narrowed, then she relaxed her shoulders and took a deep breath. "In a few years, you'll be free from all of it. Do this, and I'll help you train. We can get your skills where they need to be for a scholarship and then you can leave this hellhole, like the rest of us. You can start fresh someplace else. Make friends. Don't you want that?"

More than Heather knew.

"It's what we all want for you." Heather turned to Erin, she nodded. Even Lauren tipped her chin. "We're friends, Cassie, and we don't want to see this one thing destroy your future."

Tears ran down Cassie's cheeks.

"We tried to save Jennifer, but we couldn't. We did everything we could. Calling the police won't help her now."

But it would give her family peace and Cassie knew what a gift that would be. Since her dad left without saying goodbye.

She bit her lip.

"So, we agree on what to do next, right?"

There was desperation in Heather's eyes, but behind that, deeper in the blue was a hint of something else. Something dangerous and animal, a fear of getting caught and losing everything.

Cassie took a deep breath and nodded.

"Say it out loud." Erin's voice held the slightest hint of a threat.

"I agree." Her voice came out small and uncertain, all wisps of bravado vanished. "We were never there."

—

Cassie parked her car at Jamie's single-level home, and ran a hand through her hair.

What a nightmare.

The warm air clung to her as she got out, and walked over to Jamie's window. With a soft rattle, she drummed her knuckles on the glass. It only took a few seconds for Jamie to raise the blinds and lift the pane. They removed the screen, something they'd been doing for three years since they'd become friends, and Cassie climbed in.

"It's midnight. I thought you were hanging with your cool new friends." Jamie kept her voice low, but the hurt and sarcasm dripped from each word.

"Please, don't start. Not tonight." Cassie kicked off her shoes and curled up on the bed.

Jamie frowned and sat beside her. "What happened?"

She shook her head. Cassie needed to be with her friend, the one person in the world who cared what happened to her, but she had no intention of recounting the night's horror. "Nothing. Really. It's just been a long day."

"Want to hear something ridiculous? It might help get your mind off whatever is bothering you."

"Please." Cassie forced a smile.

"My mom decided it's vital to my high school experience for me to go to the homecoming dance."

"You? At a school function?" She wondered what Jamie's dyed black hair would look like pulled up in a French twist.

"Yeah, I know. It's lame." Jamie frowned. "It's almost four weeks away, but apparently I have to find a date immediately, and figure out where to eat dinner, and buy a dress."

Cassie cocked an eyebrow. "A dress?"

"Yeah, yeah. I know, the apocalypse is near, right? Me in a dress. But hey, you're going to have to do the same." Jamie nudged Cassie. "You're not deserting me in my moment of need."

"You make it sound so tempting." She frowned as she studied her hands. They trembled.

Jamie noticed. She took them in her own, the warmth spreading to Cassie's chest. "You're clearly not okay. Talk to me."

Cassie closed her eyes to keep the tears in. "I

can't."

"Cass." Jamie wrapped her arm around Cassie and pulled her close. Cassie rested her head on Jamie's shoulder. They'd held each other before, a few times in the past when life became unbearable. When Jamie's parents yelled or Cassie's nightmares of being left by her dad flared up, but it'd become more regular, more comfortable to lean on each other.

"I did something, Jamie. Something I can't take back and I'm scared."

"It's okay," Jamie cooed, but it only made the tears race down Cassie's face.

"No, I really messed up this time. I'm a fuck up. It doesn't matter where I'm sent to live or with which relative. I destroy everything I touch." She pushed up and scooted away. "I shouldn't have even come here tonight."

Why was she such a poison? All her life, everything she loved fell apart.

Jamie cupped Cassie's chin. "Hey, you are not a fuck up. Your dad, he's the one who neglected you and ran off to start a new family, okay? And your mom's drinking—"

"Stop."

"— wasn't your fault."

Cassie shook her head. "I'm never going to be free. I'm never going to leave this place."

"Why do you have to leave this place to be free?" Jamie let her hands fall to the lap. "You always say that, but would it really be so bad if what you're looking for wasn't a thousand miles away? Cass, you're a tough person. You don't need to run away from your problems."

Cassie wiped her tears and climbed to her feet. "I'm sorry. I shouldn't have come here."

"Don't be like that." Jamie stood. "Tell me what happened tonight. What did those girls do to you?"

"Why do you always think it's them?" More venom came out than she wanted, but she was exhausted. "Sorry."

"Come on. Talk to me. You know you'll spill eventually." Jamie offered a smile.

"This is crazy." Pressure pinched the back of Cassie's neck as she steadied her breath.

"Hey, it's okay." Jamie sat back down and patted the spot beside her. "Come on."

Cassie knew she should be strong. She desperately wanted to hold back the emotion, keep it locked inside and shield her best friend from everything, but instead she sat down. The words tumbled from her lips. "We did something. Me and Erin and Heather and Lauren. Something terrible that we can't undo, and now there's a chance I'm gonna go to jail, which is pretty much where I belong after tonight. Just like my mom. The two of us, we could be cellmates, wouldn't that be great?"

"Whoa, slow down. Start from the beginning."

Cassie inhaled deep and then let the whole story out. Once she finished, she held her breath and watched a wave of emotion run over her best friend's face.

"Shit." Jamie ran a hand through her long hair. "So...I mean, you're sure she was..." She took her pointer finger and dragged it across her neck.

"Yeah. Positive." Cassie's stomach twisted.

"I guess we need to figure out who was in the office."

"You believe me?" Cassie's voice rose.

"Doors don't just open by themselves." Jamie twirled a strand of hair around her finger. "I don't get it. Something feels off."

"Gee, you think?"

Jamie rolled her eyes. "No, seriously. There's too many questions without answers."

"That's what I tried to tell Heather."

"Heather's a trash person with an IQ of fifteen. I think we need to investigate."

Cassie shook her head. "It's too dangerous. What if the person who was in the office starts to hunt us? Haven't you seen any horror movies? This is the part where the killer starts offing people one-by-one."

"Yeah, except as far as we know, the oven murdered Jennifer." Jamie huffed. "I think you're

36

safe from an appliance." She took Cassie's hand and gave it a squeeze. "There is one thing I agree with Heather about. I don't think you should call the cops. Not yet."

"Seriously?"

"Let's figure out the whole story. See what we're facing, then make a decision, okay? We have Home Ec first period, so we'll at least be there for the initial reaction."

Dread flavored Cassie's saliva with a cold bitterness. "Oh, God. I can't believe I actually have to go back into that room."

"It's okay. I'll be with you." Jamie gave another squeeze.

Uncertainty crept through Cassie, but she nodded. "Okay. Let's handle this your way."

"Good." Jamie smiled. "We'll figure it out together."

# Chapter Four

## Emily Bower

Emily Bower did her best impression of a normal human being. She dabbed liquid foundation over the dark bags beneath her eyes, swooshed away the vodka scent with some mouthwash, and managed to arrive at work on time.

She downed a cup of coffee—so quickly the liquid burned her throat—as first period filed into the classroom.

Cassie paused at the threshold, face pale and eyes darting toward the oven.

Nothing remained. No one would ever find the body or Jennifer's truck. At least, she hoped.

Or did she? It'd only been one night, but she already paced a flattened pattern into her living room's carpet. Guilt teased her frayed nerves. She closed her eyes and leaned against the demonstration table.

A vision etched into the back of her eyelids. Jennifer's body, bits of flesh and burnt bone dropping to the floor as Emily lifted her from the oven.

"Everything okay, Ms. Bower?"

She opened her eyes, ignored the ramped thumping of her pulse and forced a smile at the short junior standing in front of her.

"Of course, Rachel. Please, take your seat."

The students piled in.

*Okay, just get through today. One class at a time.*

"It's omelet day." Her voice cracked. She cleared her throat and stood. "Please pair up and grab the eggs from the refrigerator."

Cassie. The girl seemed okay, all things

38

considered. Jamie stayed close, but that wasn't unusual, and they kept their heads down, focused on the lesson.

Twice last night, Emily threw up while cleaning the oven. Her stomach flipped at the sight of the appliance, but at least she had nothing left to hurl.

Cassie swayed on her feet, her body sagging, but Jamie quickly embraced her and helped her stand straight.

Emily took a step toward them, then paused. Any other day, she would insist Cassie sit down, maybe even go to the nurse, but today she turned her back and preoccupied herself with the other students.

So what if Cassie passed out? Wasn't she just as much to blame for what happened last night?

No, not exactly. But at least no one called the cops—there'd be police all over the school by now if they had. Which meant Cassie and her friends had no intention of getting caught, and at least that's one thing they had in common.

Emily busied herself for the rest of class until the bell rang. Cassie scurried out without looking up from the floor. They'd made it. At least, for now.

Two more periods passed with Emily mimicking her normal routine and then she finally got to rest during her planning period. Usually, she stayed in her office, but the thought of spending one more minute in the same room as that oven sent a ripple of panic through her gut. She hurried down the hallway to the teacher's lounge where she poured a fresh cup of coffee and rested on the fluffy couch.

"I heard what happened last night."

Emily froze. Fear, stark and vivid, stabbed her chest as the High Priestess' voice came from behind. She swallowed the knot in her throat, refused to turn to meet the eyes of her leader.

"How did you find out?" Had she made a mistake disposing the remains? No, impossible. She took the body to the woods and burned it to ash, bones, and teeth.

Bones and teeth that were now buried deep.

"Was it a secret? You don't need to be ashamed. Witchcraft is an art, not something to be mastered overnight. A few failed attempts are expected."

Air deflated from her lungs as she nodded, her mind spinning with realization. "Yes, the soufflé. It didn't go as expected."

"It's okay." The High Priestess placed her warm hands on Emily's neck, gave a light squeeze. "I know you probably think this time constraint is silly, but it's important to see how you respond under pressure. We need to know we can always rely on you, even in times of distress. Understand?"

Emily nodded and felt the hands fall away, sensed movement, and the opening of the lounge door.

"Was that all, Ms. Bower? Anything else I need to know other than the failed soufflé?"

Emily shoved her hands in her lap to keep them from trembling. She could come clean right now, tell everything that happened and beg for help. Surely the High Priestess knew a way out of this mess. Maybe not to bring Jennifer back, which never ended well according to stories she'd heard, but a spell to keep suspicion away. But a confession meant the end of her dream. No sisterhood. No coven. No family.

More loneliness.

No, she needed to toughen up. The worst had already happened. Whatever the fallout, she could handle it.

"No, nothing else."

"Very well. Keep practicing. The full moon will be here before you know it." The door closed and Emily slumped over, head cradled in her hands, squeezing back tears.

# Chapter Five

## Erin Weebly

Erin Weebly hated weight training days. Once a

week, after school let out, the soccer team lifted in the small weight room off the main gym. She preferred outdoor practice, on the field where she shined, instead of being cooped up and surrounded by the foul stench of her teammate's sweat. Today, her whole body twitched as if ants crawled just beneath her skin's surface and she longed to be sprinting with the grass under her cleats.

"Braden officially asked me to the homecoming dance." Heather picked up a free weight and started lifting it above her head. "Of course, we were always going to go, but I wanted him to put some effort into popping the question."

"Sure." Erin stopped rowing on the machine and wiped the beads of sweat with the back of her hand.

"And I made him promise to get Matt to ask you."

"Heather." Heat flashed her cheeks. Matt barely looked at Erin, even though she'd been crushing on him since last year when they were paired up as lab partners in Physics class.

"And he's gonna force Elliot to ask Cassie."

Erin's face soured. "Why'd you do that?"

"Oh, come on. She's one of us now, whether we like it or not."

Erin frowned and crossed her arms over her chest. "I didn't realize you were into charity cases."

"Look," Heather set the weights on the floor, "we

need to stick together, okay? And the closer we are to Cassie, the more control we have over her. I mean, we're already losing our grip on Lauren. Did she call you last night too? Yeah? She told me that Jennifer's hungry, whatever the hell that means."

"Ugh, don't remind me." Erin shivered despite the stuffy humidity of the weight room.

"We'll keep an eye on her, but we can't afford two nut jobs." Heather tilted her head toward Cassie who stood by the water cooler, refilling her thermos. "Lauren's always been sensitive. She can't even watch a scary movie, so of course she's stunned. It'd be weird if she wasn't, right? But Cassie. Well, we don't know a whole ton about her. What if she's plotting against us? What if she goes to the cops?"

"So, we keep her close." Erin nodded. "Yeah, okay. But does she have to come to homecoming? She'll ruin everything with her weirdness."

"It'll be fine." Heather wiped her face with a towel.

"Okay, ladies. Let's wrap it up." Coach clapped her hands. "Good job today. Tomorrow, we're back on the field. Go grab your stuff from the locker rooms. Erin, would you mind doing one final wipe down of the machines before heading out?"

"Sure."

"Great, just let me know when you're done. I'll be in my classroom."

Erin gave Heather a wave, who followed her mom out of the weight room. Cassie locked eyes with Erin, but quickly let the gaze fall and hurried away.

Heather was right, as usual. Lauren would be fine with time. But who knows what Cassie was capable of?

Erin sighed and looked at herself in the mirror, admiring the muscles she'd gained with efforts on the soccer field. She turned and ran her hand down her stomach.

"Gag, gross." She sucked it in. Her mom hid diet pills under the bathroom sink. Time to rummage through the stash. Again.

Erin turned but her foot caught on something, sending her falling face first to the weight room floor. Her spread hands absorbed the worst of the impact.

"Shit." Pain shot up her calf. Heather had forgotten to put away her weights. She groaned and sat up, cradling her ankle. A puffy swollen ball started to form.

With a gentle touch, she pushed on the flesh and winced. A little sore, but nothing seemed broken.

Ice. She needed ice. If she stopped the swelling now, maybe she could be back on the field by the end of the week.

The cafeteria sat along the same hall as the gym,

just a short trek. She got up and hopped to the gym doors. Her sneaker squeaked on the waxy tile floor. An eerie feeling washed through her as she entered the hallway.

The halogen lights shined from above, casting fluorescent white against the cinderblock walls and slate grey lockers.

"Hello?" Erin looked towards the cafeteria. Emptiness. Her pulse quickened, but she started moving anyway.

Hop. Breathe. Hop. Breathe.

"Erin." A soft voice fluttered past her ear.

Pain flexed her ankle as she spun around, standing on both feet. "Who said that?"

Her heart raced as she turned back around.

Only emptiness answered.

"Coach? Heather?" She craned her neck left to right. "Hello?"

She shuffled on, the pain waning as her panic grew. The Home Ec room occupied the closest corner—lights on.

Jennifer's charred face flashed before Erin's like a hologram, the melting skin and flaming hair. Erin squeezed her eyelids together tight, but her mind replayed Jennifer's wide gaze, filled with terror and agony.

"No, it wasn't my fault." Erin opened her eyes and pedaled in reverse, her sore foot dragging painfully.

Heather was the one hell bent on putting Jennifer in her place. It was her idea.

And then Jennifer had to go into the Home Ec room, then what? Climbed into the oven?

Who does that?

The lights flickered. The air grew sour, but with a tart undertone. The Home Ec door cracked open. Erin froze as a buttery aroma filled the hall, the one scent she loved but deprived herself of. The bitter and sweet smells gliding toward her, reminding her of what she gave up, her one and only food allergy.

Bread.

Her mouth watered. Her feet took a tiny step, but she paused.

Returning to the scene of the crime seemed like a bad idea. Although, Cassie took Home Ec and had to be in that room earlier that day. Surely if Cassie could muster up the guts to spend time in there, Erin could at least poke her head in and see what was going on.

Maybe she'd find a clue, a way to figure out what happened to Jennifer's body or who was watching them. She'd be a hero.

Okay, maybe not a hero. She did get Jennifer killed.

But at least she would have something to tell Heather and maybe that would make her want to hang out more, without that loser Cassie.

She pushed the door open.

Ms. Bower wasn't there.

But the oven light shined.

"Heather, if this is a joke, it isn't funny." Erin forced strength into her voice, but it came out small and wavering. The scent caused her stomach to rumble.

*Ding.*

The oven door opened.

A huge golden croissant whipped its rounded arms out of the oven, gripping either side. It propelled itself forward and popped out, rolling to the floor.

"What the hell?" Erin took a step in reverse, blinking, a sense of confusion spiraling through her mind.

It sat on the ground, the size of a retriever and just as golden. Flaky and steaming, it was more than perfect. Erin's stomach growled again while her brain tumbled with uncertainty. She chewed her lower lip and found herself taking another tiny step forward. It'd been two years since her gluten allergy diagnosis. Most people in her family thought it was bogus, just a made-up condition from her doctor. But Erin knew eating even a small dinner roll would have her bent over in agony for hours.

Still, she seemed drawn to this croissant. That

scent was heaven. The little bubbles rising atop the buttery golden contours. Everything in her mind screamed for her to run away, but the lore of perfect flaky pastry overtook reasoning skills. Her hands trembled as she reached for it, dropping to one knee—her foot barked, but she didn't feel it. Just as her fingertips came into reach, the croissant swung around and growled.

A gooey mouth opened with tendrils of uncooked dough, just like her Jack-O-Lantern at Halloween when she didn't clean out all the guck before cutting the mouth holes. Two small dough eyes, burnt and black, narrowed and focused on her.

"Bonjour, mon amie."

It lunged and clomped down on Erin's hand. A scream erupted from her core, echoed off the walls, as the moist, slimy dough wrapped around her wrist. Heat radiated down her arm, sizzling from the croissant's mouth and burning her bare flesh. Erin jumped up and flailed her arm, the croissant staying attached until she slammed it against the wall, causing the pastry to release and plop to the ground.

Blood streaked her hand and bits of skin around the open wounds were charred black. Another scream as Erin jetted out of the room, her ankle holding up under the pressure, as she raced back toward the gym.

"Mademoiselle!" the French-accented croissant

called after her.

Her hair whipped her face as she looked over her shoulder. It teetered on its two round edges, scampering after her like a seesaw hellbent on revenge. She reached the door, hurried through and slammed it shut.

"What the fuck?" Her chest heaved.

The door flung open, the croissant's mouth pulled into a frown.

"Tsk tsk tsk. That was very rude."

"This isn't happening." Erin shook her head, stumbling away from the impossible thing.

The croissant laughed, a low rumble that spat tiny specks of dough through the air. "You and your friends have no idea of the trouble you cooked up. But don't worry, Mademoiselle, you won't be around for the worst of it." It laughed then: *hon hon hon.*

It wrapped one of its edges around her sore ankle and tugged.

"No, please!" Erin screamed and fell to the ground. It climbed up her legs and straddled her chest, her arms now pinned by her side. Each squirm only seemed to lock her tighter in place.

The croissant opened its mouth. A roar erupted, sending luscious smelling wedges of dough onto Erin's face. She screamed and kicked, tossed her head from side-to-side, but the dough rained down along her forehead.

And then it started to burn.

Her cheeks flamed. The croissant wedged her mouth open with its edge and despite everything, desire danced along her taste buds as the sweet and creamy dough pushed further inside. It'd been so long since she'd had a croissant that her mouth opened wider, hypnotized by the delicious buttery goodness. The edge pushed past her teeth, past the back of her throat. The croissant ignored her wails, as panic overtook her brief crazy pleasure. It muffled her cries with its body as it slid further down her esophagus and into her gut.

# Chapter Six

## Cassie Adler

Cassie pushed the baked beans around her plate. Her grandmother set aside her own dinner and lit a cigarette, the tobacco scent immediately filling the room.

"You've been quiet lately."

Cassie shrugged.

Grandma tipped her head back and exhaled a steady puff of smoke. "I heard about a girl that went missing. The one on your soccer team. Jennifer, right?"

Cassie froze. "What are you talking about?"

"Her mom was in the grocery store causing a scene. She started handing out flyers with her girl's picture on them, demanding answers as if there was some big conspiracy going on. Girl probably just ran away, maybe holding up with her boyfriend or something like that."

"She didn't have a boyfriend," Cassie mumbled.

"Anyways, she said the cops won't help her yet. Not enough time has passed so she took matters into her own hands. Apparently, she's been marching up and down Main Street, knocking on doors, asking for information. Can't say I blame her, but some people just act up and run off."

Cassie frowned. "Thinking of anyone in particular? My dad, maybe? I know how much you love reminding me that he left."

Her grandma clenched her fist "You know, you have a little attitude on you. Just like your mother."

"Why do you always have to say bad things about her?" Cassie looked down at her lap, twisted the cord of her soccer shorts. "She's been in jail over a year, doing her time. Maybe when she gets out, you can cut her some slack instead of making her feel like a loser. Did you ever think that she could use a little help? What if you were actually nice to her? Maybe she'd stop the drinking once and for all."

She looked up into the dark eyes of her mom's

mother, the woman forced to accept Cassie into her home when no one else was left. For a second, Cassie thought a flicker of sadness cast a shadow over the woman's face, but it passed too quickly to be sure and was replaced by a crisp narrow stare and wrinkled forehead.

"Don't talk back to me. You think you know everything, don't you?"

Cassie chewed her lower lip and looked down at her plate.

It hadn't always been this way. She and her parents used to live on the other side of town, a small one-story brick house with two tiny bedrooms. Grandma came for dinner most weekends, and Cassie actually liked her back then. Her grandmother's personality still prickled most people, but Cassie admired the older woman's grit. She'd hoped some of that fighting spirit would rub off on her mom when things went south, but Cassie's mom only wilted under the pressure and Grandma turned hard as stone after Mom's first arrest.

The doorbell rang and she pushed her chair back, relief washing the frustration away. "That's Jamie. I asked her to come over and help me study History."

"You'll need all the help you can get." Grandma frowned. "Just like your mother."

Cassie ignored the jab and hurried to let in Jamie. They made a straight path to Cassie's' room, locking the door behind them.

Jamie dropped her backpack on the floor and sat on the bed. "You look tired."

"Gee, thanks." Cassie frowned.

"Sorry, but maybe this will perk you up. I've been doing some thinking about Jennifer." She opened her bag, pulled out a spiral notebook and flipped it open. A long list of teachers filled the spaces. "Every teacher is a suspect, because they all have access to the school afterhours. Ms. Bower, of course, is the prime suspect since it's her room, but I think the bigger question isn't who, but why."

The phone rang.

"Hold that thought." Cassie reached over to her nightstand and picked it up.

"Cassie...oh, God, something's happened..."

"Lauren?" Cassie's eyes widened at the sound of her friend's small voice. "What's going on? Are you okay?"

"We pissed her off and now, something is happening. Erin's first, but none of us are safe."

The words barely registered, her mind reeled. "I don't understand. What happened to Erin?"

"She's dead."

Cassie's jaw dropped. "That doesn't make sense. I just saw her at soccer practice."

Jamie mouthed words. *What's going on?*

Cassie shook her head and pressed the phone

receiver closer to her ear.

"Heather called me. She said they found Erin's body in the gym, lying on the floor. Her mouth covered in crumbs. They won't know for sure what killed her unless her parents do an autopsy, which I don't even know if they'll want to do. I mean, can you imagine? Some medical examiner cutting up your kid and taking out the insides?"

"So then how do they think she died?" Cassie swallowed creeping bile.

Jamie's eyes widened. She gasped and covered her mouth.

"Based on the crumbs, they're thinking food allergy. Did you know Erin couldn't eat gluten?"

"Um, no. I guess I didn't."

"But surely, Erin knew about the allergy, right? So why would she eat something that would hurt her? Don't you see?"

Cassie's chest tightened. "See what? That Erin had a moment of weakness and ate some carbs?"

"No, no. You don't get it." Lauren's voice held a tremor. "Heather's scared. She won't admit it, of course, but it's obvious. Don't you see, Cassie? It can't just be a coincidence. Two days ago, Jennifer. And now, Erin. We have to pay for what we've done."

"No, that's..." Cassie's head swirled. "Look, just take a breath and try to calm down."

"Yeah, sure. Whatever you say." Lauren's voice

lowered. "But I saw her."

"Who?"

"Jennifer. I saw her the night we killed her. When I got home, she stood in my bedroom."

"That's impossible."

"Her body...oh, God, the smell..." Lauren sobbed while Cassie held her breath. "She said she was hungry. Now, do you see? She's hungry for revenge."

"Lauren, do you need some help? Do you want me to come over?"

"Take care of yourself, Cassie. We all need to watch out for ourselves now." And with those words, Lauren hung up.

"Shit." Cassie slammed the receiver down.

Jamie leaned with her hands on her knees. "What happened?'"

Cassie chewed her thumbnail as Lauren's words replayed in her mind.

"Erin died."

"Holy shit."

"I guess she had an allergic reaction or something."

"Oh my God, that's awful." Jamie stood and wrapped her arms around Cassie in a soft hug. "I mean, I never liked her, but I didn't want the bitch to die."

"This is crazy. I can't believe she's gone. And Lauren's lost her mind, talking about ghosts and revenge, but what if she's right?"

Jamie pulled back.

"Not about the ghost, I know that's nuts, but about the revenge. You said it's not *the who*, but *the why* that's important, right? Well, what if *the why* got Erin killed?"

"Whoa, take a step back. Who said she was killed?"

Cassie shriveled into herself as she dropped to the bed. "Lauren did. I realize she isn't exactly the most credible person at the moment, but she made a good point. If Erin knew she had an allergy, why eat the food that would make her sick?"

Jamie twirled her hair around her finger and pursed her lips.

Cassie's hands trembled. "I think we're in real danger. Me, Lauren, and Heather. What do I do? Who do I trust with all of this?"

"Me." Jamie sat down and wrapped her arm around Cassie's shoulder. "You can always trust me."

# Chapter Seven

## Emily Bower

Emily stood at Erin's locker. Her stomach sank as she looked down at the small shrine of flowers and photos crowded on the floor. Two days had passed since Erin's death, but it'd take months before the students recovered. They walked by with their heads hung low, whispers hissing.

A food allergy.

Yeah, right.

"Such a shame." Audrey Landry stepped beside her, a plastic Tupperware container in hand. "First, Jennifer Shipley runs away and now Erin's gone. This school can't take much more tragedy."

"I know." It's all Emily could muster. At least Erin's death seemed to take way the sting of Jennifer's disappearance. Small town gossip filtered to Emily over the past few days, and she'd learned that the cops put out a missing person report, but they had no leads. Apparently, they think she ran away, bur her mom refused to accept that theory.

Wise woman.

Every muscle in Emily's body ached from fatigue. Stress weighed her down as the last few days played on repeat in her brain. She shook her head and ran a hand down her face.

"I'm sorry that I won't be able to make our meeting tonight."

"Huh?"

Audrey leaned a little closer. "You know, our *meeting*. I left you a message on your answering machine."

"Oh, right." Code for another spell lesson. "It's okay." She'd forgotten all about it.

"But I made you some brownies." Audrey handed over the Tupperware. "I figure you could use a little pick me up after our last get together and I know chocolate is your favorite."

"Thanks." She cracked open the top and inhaled the sweet scent. "Chocolate makes everything better."

"I agree. Keep your chin up, okay? It'll all work out in the end." Audrey smiled and walked down the hall, leaving Emily to consider her third period class.

She spotted Lauren in the hallway. At least, the girl looked like the shell of Lauren. Her tangled hair hung down her back, she wore baggy sweatpants and a hoodie, but her skinny arms poked out the sleeves. Emily imagined if she tried to wrap her fingers around the girl's wrist, she'd be able to touch her middle finger to her thumb. Her cheekbones jutted from beneath her skin and a hollowness sucked back her eyes, casting dark shadows around the sockets.

Emily sucked in a breath. She forced her feet to move, fingers gripping the container of brownies as she approached.

"Hello, Lauren."

Lauren jumped and spun, her eyes wide.

Emily offered a smile, but her guts twisted. "Sorry to startle you. I just wanted to come say hi and see how you're doing."

Lauren's eyebrows pinched together. "Why?"

"Just concerned, that's all. I heard you and Erin were friends and I wanted to check in. See how you're holding up." When she got no response, Emily shoved the brownies toward Lauren. "Anyways, I thought you might like these."

Lauren frowned.

"They're just brownies. My friend, Mrs. Landry, gave them to me to cheer me up, but I think maybe you could use them more than me."

"Thanks." Lauren took the container, her eyes downcast, away from Emily.

"Well, okay then." Emily turned and headed to class, a small satisfaction growing in her chest. She'd done something tiny to help someone, which had always been the goal of teaching. Maybe it wasn't too late. Maybe she could become the teacher she always wanted to be.

A boy with a DiscMan in hand and headphones over his ears bumped Emily's shoulder.

"Hey, watch it, bitch." Then he took off down the hall before she could open her mouth.

The thoughts of goodwill evaporated.

Maybe she'd work on a potion to shut up annoying teenagers. The thought warmed her as she returned to her classroom.

—

It'd been an hour since the final bell rang. Emily finished inputting grades into the computer and gathered her things. She checked the ovens, made sure the appliances were turned off, and went to lock the door. Every day spent teaching in the classroom got a little easier and for the first time since that night, a bit of hope peaked through the darkness.

"Going home?" The High Priestess stood in the doorway, hands on her hips.

Other members of the coven stepped around the High Priestess and entered the room. Mrs. Washington, the Algebra teacher, followed by Ms. Bates, who taught Biology, stepped to one side of Emily, while Mrs. Reynolds, an English teacher, stepped to the other.

Audrey shuffled into the room, head down, hands folded in front of her.

"Is there something you need from me?" A wave of panic washed over Emily, but she rolled her shoulders and forced her back to remain stiff. "It's not time for my test, right? You said I had until the full moon."

"I'm afraid we're past all the silly test business." The High Priestess sighed and shook her head. "You've made a mess."

"A mess?"

"Please. Don't pretend to not understand. We

60

know the oven held left over magic from your failed spell and then consumed that girl." The High Priestess narrowed her eyes. "And we know you tried to cover it up, which made things exponentially worse. You can't even imagine the damage you've caused."

Emily swallowed the lump in her throat. How did they find out? She'd been so careful to cover her tracks. "I'm so sorry. I never meant to hurt anyone."

"And yet, you did. Can you imagine what would happen if people found out the truth? You're the reason people will never accept who we are. You've given us all a bad name by your ignorance and now that poor girl's soul is trapped in that oven, conjuring up demon desserts to vanquish her enemies. Are you happy with yourself?"

Emily's mouth dropped open. Shock rippled through her body as realization settled in her bones. "Jennifer's soul is trapped?"

"Apparently." The High Priestess smoothed her hair and let out a deep breath. "She baked up some sort of pastry that choked Erin to death."

"What?" The room spun as Emily gripped the counter.

"But it's not your problem. We'll clean up your mess and the coven will only grow stronger over time."

"Please," Emily pressed her hands together as if

she were praying, "give me another chance. Don't kick me out before I have the opportunity to prove myself. I know I messed up, but being one of you means everything to me." She looked around the circle, meeting the eyes of her fellow teachers, of her soon-to-be sisters if only they'd hear her pleas.

Audrey lifted her face, her profile strong and rigid. "High Priestess, what if we let Emily fix it? If she can't, then all the blame will fall on her shoulders. We can banish her from the group, as you wish, and set her up to handle the practical consequences of her actions."

A flash of sirens and jail cells flickered in Emily's mind.

"But, if she undoes the spell and finds peace for Jennifer's soul, she earns a spot in our circle and our friendship. No more tests, no more trials. She'll be one of us."

The High Priestess folded her arms over her chest. "Fine, but since you vouched for her, she's your responsibility. The two of you do whatever it takes to put a lid on this situation. If it goes well, Emily gets what she wants. If it goes poorly, you both will be out of the coven and handed over to the cops. And if you try to rat us out—" She held her hand up and curled her fingers into her palms. As she did this, Emily's tongue twisted, and pain shot through her mouth.

*She's going to snap off my tongue!*

And just as quickly as it came, the agony faded, and the High Priestess stepped back. "You better thank your friend." She looked to Audrey and snarled. "You two are in this together."

Then she turned and walked away, the others following.

"Thanks." Emily offered a small smile.

"It's the best chance you'll have at achieving your dream, but we need to get to work. I have a spell that might help if you're willing to try."

Emily nodded. "I'll try anything. Whatever it takes."

# Chapter Eight

## Lauren Fisher

Lauren pushed open the front door of her house, dropped her bookbag on the kitchen counter, pried open the Tupperware lid, and shoved a brownie in her mouth.

Sweet chocolate. The solution to all the world's problems.

Erin always cautioned Lauren about the dangers of too much sugar. Big butt and flappy arms, which in Erin's world meant no one would ever ask her to

Homecoming, but Lauren didn't care about any of that now.

Erin died and Jennifer killed her.

Somehow, it had happened. Just like somehow, Jennifer's ghost appeared at the foot of Lauren's bed the night of the incident. Not that anyone believed her.

With the first brownie still soggy in her mouth, she shoved in another, opened the fridge, popped open a can of soda and chugged it down. Her stomach rumbled, demanding more.

She grabbed a third brownie and headed toward the living room. "Mom? Dad? Robbie?"

No answer. She paused and called out again.

No one home.

*Okay, that's not unusual. Sometimes Mom and Dad work late. But Robbie?*

Her freshman brother usually took the bus home so he could ride with his friends, but where was he? He should be home by now, playing video games and driving Lauren crazy. Did he go over to someone's house to hang out?

Or did Jennifer get him?

"Hello?" She set the brownie on the coffee table. Everything seemed in order. The family portrait centered the wall, each member smiling bright into the camera with their backs straight and hands folded in their laps. The couch and recliner rested against the wall opposite the television and her dad's tea mug sat on the coffee table, left behind from his morning routine. Same as always.

Jitters bounced around her stomach as she did a mental intake of the room.

She hated this version of herself, the one that jumped at the slightest sound and barely managed to get out of bed in the morning. Darkness followed each step, burdening her and threatening to overpower with each passing moment. Lauren's parents forced her to go to school, tried to get her to resume some sort of normal routine, but how could she think of school or homecoming or soccer when a ghost wanted her dead? Still, she knew her parents wouldn't let this behavior go on forever. Despite their overbearing nature, they loved Lauren and she wanted to at least try to make them happy. Whispers of taking Lauren to a therapist escaped her dad's lips late last night—he thought Lauren wasn't paying attention.

But no one could help her.

The hairs on her arm stood at attention as the air cooled.

"Fuck this." She'd go to Heather's house for a few hours until her parents got home.

"Hungry!" A voice boomed from the kitchen and caused a jolt to ripple down her spine.

She didn't waste time. Lauren ran toward the

front door, panic rising, sapping the air from her lungs. Thunderous footsteps thumped from behind. Just as her hands scraped the front door, a large arm wrapped around her waist and pulled her back.

"Must eat."

Lauren gasped as she twisted in the creature's grip until they were face-to-face. A monster, about six feet tall, made solely out of brownie, squeezed her midsection. It had no real form, just a blob of chocolate brownie bits piled high and squished together with squid-like appendages for arms and legs. It tipped its bulbous head to the side. "Food?"

"No." She forced her voice to grow louder. "I'm not food."

The monster tilted its head to the other side and leaned closer. Heat radiated from its crumbling skin as if it registered her with its nut cluster eyes. The damned thing smelled so good Lauren's mouth watered even as tears began to surface.

"Food." The decision was made. The monster's mouth opened, at first just a few inches, then it widened like an anaconda's unhinged jaw. Lauren squirmed in terror, writhing and kicking, but it didn't matter. The monster lifted her up and tipped its head back.

"Don't eat me!"

It ignored her plea and shoved her headfirst into its mouth. Her skull fit snug, as if someone wrapped a chocolate scented scarf around her face. She saw nothing but brown as she opened her mouth and tried to scream once more, but the monster's insides absorbed the noise as chocolate crumbs packed against her teeth.

She swallowed them away and then the creature swallowed, and her body inched forward, pushed by an unseen force that kept moving her deeper along the monster's entrails.

*So, this is how I'll die. Death by chocolate.*

She wanted to laugh but settled for a soft moan as the fight dissolved from her. She relaxed, no longer fighting the force as it pushed her into what she imagined to be the creature's stomach.

This is what she deserved.

The stomach cavity offered enough space for her to curl her knees to her chest. Warmth wrapped her entire body as sweat slicked her skin.

At least she'd die surrounded by her favorite food.

Might as well have another bite.

She opened her mouth and chomped down. A groan slipped from the monster and the sound rumbled around her. A tiny flame of hope sparked in her chest. She took another bite. The same groan passed through the stomach wall.

*This might work.*

Except her stomach tightened at the thought of

one more chocolate bite.

*Come on. You can do it. Just eat your way to freedom.*

Lauren opened her mouth, took a huge chunk and forced it down her throat until enough bites were taken to push open the outer wall. Her fingers slipped through and light shined in.

The monster howled and started wiggling, but Lauren didn't care. She balled her fists and started punching at the monster's skin. Nausea swept through her as sweat dripped from her face.

*Don't pass out. If you pass out, you're dead. Keep going, you can do this.*

She punched over and over, the monster groaning with each blow until her hand busted out. The creature howled as Lauren wiggled her arm through the hole, loosening the crumbly brownie bits just enough for her head to crest the surface.

Lauren pushed as hard as she could until her entire face emerged from the monster's gut. She took a deep breath, then another, looking up into the face of a stunned and confused brownie creature. Her shoulder pushed upward and out, busting through followed by her other shoulder. The monster dropped to its knees and watched as Lauren wiggled the rest of her body free.

"Food?"

"No." Lauren heaved as she leaned against the

coffee table, the creature now nothing more than a heap of chocolate. "I'm not food!"

Then she gripped its head and twisted it clean off, dropping it onto her lap.

"Honey?"

She looked up and saw her mom standing in the kitchen doorway, a bag of groceries in hand, utter terror written on her face.

# Chapter Nine

## Emily Bower

"Are you sure about this?" Emily stood at the wire fence. Goats peppered the field on the opposite side, eating grass and enjoying the weekend sunshine. A waft of dirt and manure flavored the air, forcing Emily to breathe through her mouth.

Plenty of farms dotted the hillsides in Rochelle, but this particular farm was known for breeding and selling goats.

"We need a tuft of its hair." Audrey passed over a pair of scissors. "You might want to get a little extra, just to be safe."

"Right." Emily took the scissors and looked over at the goats. They weren't the little things she'd encountered at a petting zoo back as a kid. These stood tall, the size of a German Shephard, with horns. One looked up and stared at Emily with his creepy vertical pupils.

"Well, go ahead." Audrey gave her a little push.

She gave a quick glance back down the hill where the farmhouse sat. No cars in the driveway, no sounds coming from inside. They'd rang the bell and banged on the door. No one answered. Hopefully, whoever owned the place would be gone long enough for Emily to collect the hair.

She straddled the top fence wire and swung her leg over, landed with a stumble. "Hey, I just want to thank you again for helping me."

Audrey shrugged. "It probably wasn't the brightest thing for me to do seeing as how I'm now ankle deep in goat poop." She snickered and Emily smiled. "I'm just glad you're getting a second chance."

"Me too." Emily frowned as one of the goats started walking closer to the fence. She took a small step forward.

"You know, I didn't make it into the coven my first try."

"Really?" Emily took another small step. The goat looked up, locked eyes for a second, and then went back to munching grass.

"I had trouble with my spells and the High Priestess wasn't sure I fit in."

"So, how'd you prove yourself?" She held up the scissors.

"It took a lot of patience and persistence. And I wish someone stuck up for me so I didn't have to waste so much time begging for more chances."

Emily looked back at Audrey. "I'm sorry that happened to you."

"At least I finally made it and you will too."

"But have you tried it? The spell, I mean."

Audrey chewed her lip for a second. "There's a first time for everything. Like you giving a goat a haircut."

"Yeah." Emily's smile faded as she took the last step up to the goat. Careful to keep her hand steady, she positioned the blade close to the fur. "Okay, now just hold still, friend."

"Hey, what are you two doing?"

Emily jerked her head up and saw an angry woman, gray hair blowing in the breeze, hustling up the hill.

The goat spun and rammed his horns into Emily's ribs.

"Shit." She flopped to the grass.

"Hurry, we have to go."

Emily winced as she got to her feet.

"You two, stop right there." The woman huffed, halting for a split second to gather her breath.

Emily hurried, put the goat in a chokehold and

snipped a chunk of hair. "I got it."

"Great, now can we get out of here?" Panic seized Audrey's words as she started to run away, down the opposite side of the hill to their car. Emily scampered over the fence and started racing, her side burning with pain.

"I'm calling the cops!" The gray hair woman made it to the top of the hill just as Emily and Audrey reached the bottom. They looked up—the woman was waving her fists in the air—and jumped into the car.

Ten minutes later, they rode down the main highway, Emily's pulse returning to normal.

"Think she really called the cops?"

"Probably, but I don't think it matters." Audrey gave a quick glance. "Think about it. Two grown women hopping a fence aren't really a threat. I doubt she saw you cut the goat's hair, not from where she was on the hill."

"Yeah, I guess." Emily sighed. "Now can we please make this potion and fix my stupid mistake before anyone else gets hurt."

"We need more ingredients."

—

They arrived at the Home Ec room just as midnight settled over the town. Emily's hand trembled as she twisted off the Mason jar's lid and allowed the bitter scent to fill the room. The black sludge bubbled, a tuft of goat hair settled on top.

"We just pour it on the oven?"

"Apparently." Audrey opened the spell book and set it on the countertop. "I'll say the spell while you drip the potion on the stovetop, okay?"

Resolve solidified Emily's stance, settling her nerves and steadying her hand.

"Ready?"

"Let's do this."

Audrey's voice droned, her words hypnotic and slow. The potion slid out of the jar like molasses, each drip collecting into a tiny pool on the stovetop. The bitterness in the air shifted, replaced with an acidic stench.

The lights flickered.

"Is that normal?"

Audrey looked around the room, her eyes wide. "Yeah, probably."

"Probably?" Fear tightened Emily's chest as Audrey refocused on the spell.

A warning voice whispered inside Emily's head.

*Run.*

But before her feet processed the command, darkness fell on the room. Emily's breath caught in the back of her throat and Audrey sucked in air.

"What do we do?" She tried to control the fear creeping through her body, pulse racing. Shadows rose from the floor and while she tried to convince herself that the shapes meant her no harm, something shifted against the back wall. "What was that?"

The lights flickered, and for a brief moment, she saw everything. The cabinets, the demonstration table, the oven.

And Jennifer.

Standing in the back corner, one eye melted away from the fire, the other narrow and glaring right at her.

The lights shut off and they stood in the dark. This time, she reached for Audrey, who gripped her sweaty hand and squeezed.

"Did you see her?" Audrey's voice came out barely above a whisper, but her fear screamed through the room. "Where'd she go?"

The silence tightened around them as Emily's eyes darted from one side of the room to the next.

The lights flickered and for another second, they stood in front of Jennifer, her hair scorched to her skull, bits of glossy flesh hanging onto her bones.

Back into darkness.

"Keep repeating the spell." Emily forced the words out as her hands fumbled for the Mason jar. Audrey's words staggered as she began to speak while Emily tipped out the final contents of the jar.

Then the lights flashed back on.

Jennifer squatted on top of the oven. Her head

tilted to the side, showing off the side of her face that no longer boasted skin. A sunken cavity carved out her cheek and where her nose should be, a flesh flap, half charred, hung limply.

"Oh, God." Emily chocked back the terror.

Audrey stuttered, but kept chanting, her voice growing in resolve with each phrase.

"Go away! Leave this oven!" But as the words erupted from Emily's core, Jennifer tilted back her head and let out a piercing wail that crumbled Emily to the floor. "Fuck!"

The scream sizzled her nerves, but she grabbed the edge of the counter and pulled herself up. Audrey's eyes blazed with horror, but her mouth kept spilling the spell and with each repetition, Jennifer howled louder.

"It's working," Emily watched as the edges of Jennifer blurred, "it's getting rid of her."

But Jennifer attacked. She dove off the oven, her entire body catapulted through the air and landed on Audrey.

"Get her off me!"

Emily leapt, wrapped her hands around Jennifer's crispy remains and flung her across the Home Ec room.

"Keep chanting." Emily cracked her knuckles, rolled back her shoulders. "I've got this."

Audrey's voice became the soundtrack as

Jennifer sprang forward. Her teeth gnashed at Emily's bare neck, but anger flared deep inside, igniting a resolve that pulsated through her clenched fist and sent a punch directly against Jennifer's ribs.

"Shit, she did something to me." Audrey dropped to her knees. "I can't..."

"Keep chanting!" Emily flung her weight forward and pinned Jennifer to the ground, ignoring the rancid odor emitting from the living corpse. "Shit, she's strong for a fucking zombie."

"Tired...so tired..."

"Audrey, get it together."

Jennifer curled back the muscles that used to be her lips and cackled with delight.

"The spell. Bind her to the school." Audrey's eyelids closed and she flopped to the floor.

"Shit." Her mind raced for the right words, willed them into the right order and screamed them at Jennifer.

Another wail. Another flicker of the lights.

And when they came back on, Jennifer was gone. Emily's chest heaved as she sat up, searched the room with her eyes and landed on Audrey, laying on the floor. She crawled over, desperation replacing her resolve as she lightly patted Audrey's cheeks.

"Come on, wake up."

Her eyelids fluttered. "Did you bind her to the room?"

"I think."

"Good enough. At least for now."

"What did she do to you?"

"I don't know for sure." Audrey groaned. "Help me up."

Emily stood, extended her hand, and pulled her friend to a standing position. "Did we do any good tonight?"

"She won't be able to leave the school property. That's better than nothing. Plus, we're alive. That's something good."

"But she can still hurt people." *And my chances of getting into the coven are still screwed.*

"It's the best we can do right now. We'll think of something else. There's got to be a way to make her weak without her manipulating us. In the meantime, we just need to keep her calm or stay out of her way or both. If possible."

Despair welled up in Emily's chest as they headed out of the school.

Nothing seemed possible anymore.

# Chapter Ten

## Cassie Adler

Cassie darted up the high school's soccer field.

School had ended a while ago, the students dispersed, teachers trickled away. Sweat beaded on her forehead and dripped down the small of her back. It felt good to be outside and doing what she loved, what she had an ounce of control over. She fired the ball and it whizzed into the goal.

Other than her, the field was empty. Coach canceled practice so everyone could attend Erin's memorial, but Cassie couldn't bring herself to go. Maybe if Lauren decided to attend, but she'd been absent, and when Cassie tried to call her home, the answering machine picked up.

She needed to let off steam, and this was the only way she knew how.

She chased after the ball. Overhead, a storm brewed, grey clouds littering the sky, holding back rain as an unsettling fog drifted over the field. She dribbled back to midfield and took a moment to catch her breath. The fog continued to crawl across the grass, wrapping around her ankles.

"Cass, you almost done?" Jamie waved from the edge of the field. "Want me to come back later?"

"No, I'm just about done. Thanks for coming. My grandma needed the car."

"No problem, but we should go before the rain."

Cassie ignored the warning, dribbled the ball toward the goal and shot. It curved into the corner of the net. "And the crowd goes wild." She raised her hands above her head and ran to collect her ball. She stopped short and said, "What in the world?"

The mist covered the ball. A sweet cherry scent filled the air and when Cassie leaned a little closer to the ground, she noticed that it wasn't white, but pale pink fog.

"Hey, Jamie? Are you seeing this?" She looked over her shoulder. Jamie stared at the ground. But the pale pink mist stopped at the edge of the field, leaving Jamie standing on untouched grass.

"What?" She took a step, but Cassie held her hand up, palm out.

"Stop, don't come closer."

A flicker of apprehension skittered over her skin as she glided her hand back-and-forth, the pale pink specks clinging to her as she raised it to her mouth.

"Hey, what's going on?"

"I think..." Cassie stuck out her tongue and dragged the tip along her palm, capturing the pink bits with her taste buds, "it's cotton candy."

"What?"

She stood, unnerved by the discovery. "The fog, it's cherry cotton candy."

Jamie stiffened. "That's not possible."

The wind shifted and the light breeze gained speed, billowing and tumbling the cotton candy into the air. Cassie kept her mouth tight, squinted against the sting of the sugar specks flicking into her eyes. Jamie shouted, but the words lodged inside the growing candy storm, distorted and vanishing as the gusts quickened.

Cassie dug her heels into the grass to keep from tumbling backwards. In front of her, a spiral twirled from the field and stretched towards the darkness above. Her breath caught. She stared, stunned and speechless, as the cotton candy tornado spiraled.

A shape morphed from within the funnel, flexing outward.

A body.

Jennifer.

Cassie screamed, ignoring the sugar assault on her throat, and bolted toward Jamie, whose eyes grew three sizes. It felt like running through snow and pink wisps clung to her bare legs like tree moss.

"Get inside your truck!" Cassie grabbed Jamie's arm and dragged once she'd crossed the field. They fumbled, then got into a rhythm, racing across the parking lot and towards the safety of Jamie's pick up.

A tendril grew from the tornado and smacked Cassie to the pavement. Laughter rumbled from the storm as she faltered to her feet and fidgeted with the passenger's door before diving onto the seat. "Drive!"

Jamie didn't need prompting. She turned the key, yanked the shifter, and slammed her foot on the gas, taking off straight through the lot. "What the fuck was that?"

Cassie's chest burned. Her breath came out in tiny staccato notes while she turned, looked out the rear window to the pink tornado swirling behind. Jennifer's body grew. Only a few feet kept them out of reach. "She's gaining on us."

"I'm going as fast as I can." Jamie white knuckled the wheel. "What's that smell?"

Cassie was about to say it probably was from her running through a cherry flavored sugar tornado, but she froze, her eyes fixed on the tiny light pink particles floating into the truck from the vents.

She slammed her hands over them, scrambled to close the air slits as the end of the parking lot grew closer.

And then pink coated everything.

The entire outside of the truck was caked in pink as cotton candy Jennifer engulfed the inside.

Jamie screamed as they reached the main road.

It stopped. The pink sugar evaporated. The vents blew cool clear air. The cherry scent faded.

"Did we kill her? Is she gone?" Jamie panted.

Cassie looked behind. The pink tornado roared over the parking lot, Jennifer's face fixed on them as they drove faster down the street.

"No. She's still there." Cassie turned back around, her heart racing.

"Why didn't she follow us?"

"I don't know. Maybe she can't."

"So what? She's trapped in the school?"

Cassie looked at her legs and dusted off the pink flakes with shaky hands. "Maybe. Hopefully."

"Shit." Jamie rubbed her chest. "I can't believe that just happened. Why food? Because it happened in the Home Ec room?"

"Apparently." She sat back, allowing the fear to wash away from her body with each deep breath. "You okay?" Cassie reached for Jamie's hand.

Jamie steered with her free hand and peeked at Cassie. "Yeah. I guess. You?"

Cassie nodded. "It takes more than cotton candy to kill me."

"So, what do we do now?"

"We need to get help. Real help."

Jamie clucked her tongue. "I have an idea."

# Chapter Eleven

## Emily Bower

Emily slid onto the stool at The Tipsy Pig Bar a small hole in the wall just south of Main Street. The bartender nodded at her arrival and fixed the usual. Cranberry vodka.

"Thanks." She took a sip and let the familiar taste glide through her, sweeping away a gnawing sensation of dread. Exhaustion took permanent residence in her muscles causing her shoulders to sag and her back to hunch forward.

At least she blended into the after-work crowd. Men and women relaxed with drinks in hand, a light buzz of conversation slowly drowning out her thoughts.

*Everything you want is out of reach. You fucked it all up.*

At least Jennifer's soul couldn't venture from school property. Surely, that counted as a step in the right direction, but what next?

Another drink.

She raised her glass and jingled the ice, waiting for the bartender to take the hint.

Behind the bar counter, a small TV perched on the ledge flashed the local news logo. A headshot of Jennifer popped up on screen.

Emily's chest tightened. "Hey, can you turn up the volume?"

But the bartender didn't hear and kept chatting with a customer on the opposite end of the counter.

"They're spreading out the search." A man with bushy eyebrows and tobacco breath sat beside her, tilted his head toward the television. "Starting to look in the woods behind the abandoned lumberyard."

"The one in the woods behind the school?"

"That's the one."

*Shit, shit, shit.*

Her pulse quickened as she stood and tossed some cash on the bar.

"Whoa, where you going?" The man's words slurred together as he watched her.

Emily lowered her head. She hurried into the parking lot, ducking into her car, and starting the engine. But her body froze.

*What if it was too late?*

*No, the guy specifically said the lumberyard's property, not the lake beside it. But it'd only be a matter of time.*

She squeezed her eyelids tight and tried to forget, but the memories tumbled from the back of her mind.

Driving to the woods behind the lumberyard.

Shoving Jennifer's body into one of the fire barrels.

The acid burning her sinuses as she puked.

Collecting the bones and ash and teeth.

More puking.

Then pushing the truck into the lake, spreading the ash, and burying the bones in various places in the woods on her walk back to the school.

Disbelief dizzied her vision as she opened her

eyes. Had she really done all that? Surely not Emily Bower, the woman who wanted nothing more than to make a difference in this community, who paid her way through college by working shitty dead end jobs and felt such elation when she got her diploma that she couldn't stop crying.

Surely that Emily didn't know the odor of a lifeless body.

Stomach acid rose in the back of her throat and she pushed open the car door just in time for chunks of a late lunch to splatter on the asphalt. It stank of vodka and Italian salad dressing. She groaned and leaned back against the driver's seat.

She could drive to the lumberyard, volunteer to help with the search. Maybe she could steer people away from all the evidence.

Or maybe it was time to go home and let it all play out. Call it quits. Accept the punishment.

An investigation.

The unveiling of the coven. Because the police would figure it all out eventually, right?

And then, finally, when it was all over, she'd end up locked away.

Prison.

The word shivered through her body as she closed the door and stared out the windshield, the evening darkening to black over the mountains.

No, she couldn't just give up.

Surely, this Emily Bower wasn't a quitter.

She started driving out toward the lumberyard, her palms sweaty against the steering wheel.

"I can do this."

Guide the other volunteers away from the lake, keep them from finding the bits of teeth and bones. Then she'd go home, drink more alcohol, pass out, and start the cycle of lies all over again tomorrow.

# Chapter Twelve

## Cassie Adler

"How do we kill a ghost?" Jamie paced her bedroom floor.

"Ghostbusters." Cassie snickered.

"Exactly."

Cassie rolled her eyes. "Jamie, I was kidding."

"Well, I'm not. We need to hire professional ghost hunters."

"I have a better idea that isn't totally insane. How about we cut off the life source?" Cassie sat on Jamie's bedroom floor, massaging a tight neck muscle. "We need to destroy the oven. That's what she's using to get her revenge. It's the food that's doing the killing. So, we get a sledgehammer and bust it up. Maybe that will kill Jennifer."

Jamie paused and cocked an eyebrow. "Or it's going to piss her off. If she lives in the oven, then we're destroying her home. What happens then? Does she find a new place to live?"

"I don't know." Cassie ran a hand through her hair. "In case you missed it, I'm making this up as I go along."

"Hey, we're going to figure this out." Jamie kept pacing. "But we definitely don't want to send a pissed off spirit out into the universe. What we need is someone who knows about all of this stuff."

"So, we're back to the Ghostbusters?" Cassie huffed. "Yeah, sure, let me just hop on the computer and do a quick search."

Jamie shrugged. "You joke, but why not? I mean, the internet has everything, right?"

Cassie frowned, but turned around and started clicking away at the keyboard. "Your search history is going to be so messed up."

Jamie leaned over her shoulder. "Holy crap, there's a whole paranormal investigation team in Virginia."

Cassie clicked on the website.

"See? I told you. Scroll down. How close are they?"

All it had was a phone number and email address. "I guess they do the whole state." She frowned. "I bet they're fake."

Jamie grinned. "Only one way to know for sure."

Cassie and Jamie worked on an email, sent it off and then went into the kitchen for some dinner. Jamie's mom and dad stood at the stove, cooking up tacos. The air laden with the heavy scent of spices and browned beef. Jamie's mom draped her arm around her daughter and gave a little squeeze.

Cassie shuffled her feet and folded her arms over her chest.

"So, what are you girls up to tonight?" Jamie's mom turned her attention back to the skillet on the stovetop.

"Oh, you know. Homework, boy talk, figuring out how to get rid of evil spirits."

Her dad chuckled. "Good luck with that."

"Boy talk?" Her mom looked at Jamie. "So, have you figured out who you're going to Homecoming with?"

"Yes. I have." Jamie moved over and locked arms with Cassie. "Mom, this is my date."

Her mom shrugged. "As long as you go. You spend too much time cooped up in this room. Go into the world. Have an adventure."

Jamie winked at Cassie. "What do you say? Should we have an adventure?"

"Sure, but only cause our lives are so incredibly boring." Cassie bit back a laugh.

They sat at the kitchen table, the food finally

ready. Cassie ate with Jamie's family often over the years—the closest thing she had to a real family.

Jamie's mom leaned over toward Cassie. "I heard about your soccer friend. Erin, wasn't that her name? I'm so sorry. How are you holding up?"

"Oh, um, okay I guess."

"That's good, sweetie. But please, if you need anything, let us know, okay?" Her mom offered a smile.

"Sure, thanks." Heat flushed Cassie's cheeks.

"Girls, I ran into Mrs. Shipley at the bank yesterday." Jamie's dad set down his taco. "She says her daughter is missing."

"Really? I thought she ran away. Isn't that what the cops say?" Jamie took a sip of water.

"Maybe, but her mom is rightfully concerned."

"That's awful." Jamie's mom sighed. "What is this world coming to?"

"I only bring it up to tell you two to be careful. Maybe she just ran off, maybe not. Just stick together, okay?"

"I can't imagine what their families are going through." Her mom shook her head.

"Wow, this is a really cheery subject." Jamie set down her glass.

"Well, we could talk about dress shopping." Her mom's eyes lit up.

Jamie groaned. "Can't we just eat in my

bedroom?"

"Fine, fine. Go." Her mom waved a hand, a smile on her face.

Jamie and Cassie grabbed their plates and retreated behind the safety of the closed door.

"They're such dorks." Jamie frowned.

"No worries." Cassie set her plate on the desk. "It's not like I can avoid what I've done. Fuck, I don't want to avoid it. It's my mistake and I need to make it right."

"Speaking of which," Jamie looked at the computer, "they replied and they're totally in." Jamie spun in the chair and smiled. "The consultation is free, but if they find a ghost, we have to pay them."

"Gee, I wonder if they'll find a ghost." Cassie frowned. "I mean, if the only way they get paid is to see a spirit..."

"Hey, a week ago, neither one of us would have considered a candy cotton tornado coming to life and nearly killing us, but here we are, so give it a chance."

"Fine. I'll talk to Heather about stealing her mom's school key."

"And she'll probably have to pay." Jamie shrugged when Cassie shot her a sideways stare. "Do you have the cash? Because I know I don't."

She sighed. "I'll see what I can do."

# Chapter Thirteen

## Cassie Adler

Cassie stood against the back wall of the Home Ec classroom as the ghost hunters stepped inside. Viv, the leader of the trio, waved her hands around as if the air were made of syrup and she needed to clear a path. Her bleached blonde hair hung past her waist, lips accentuated by brown liner, a short leather skirt showing off curvy hips.

"This is so stupid." Heather dropped into a chair and folded her arms over her chest. "I can't believe you talked me into this."

"Do you have a better idea?" Jamie smirked, her hands balled into fists and poised on her sides.

Heather frowned and looked toward Jamie. "You shouldn't even be here. Lauren should, not you."

"Yeah, well, have you been able to get her on the phone because every time I try, there's no answer," Cassie said.

"We agreed not to tell anyone." Heather stared daggers at Jamie.

Her protest had been repeated consistently and loudly for the past two days, since Cassie called and explained they needed the key to the school. And three hundred dollars.

"We agreed not to go to the cops and I didn't." Cassie sighed. "Just sit there and be quiet."

Heather's nostrils flared. Jamie stifled a laugh.

"Yes, a spirit exists and it's extremely angry." Viv stopped in the center of the room and faced the oven.

"Way to go Sherlock." Heather mumbled.

Jamie flashed her a warning stare.

"It's okay. You don't need to believe for it to be true." Viv took a deep breath, rolled her shoulders. "Reiko, are you set up?"

The short round woman with spikey black hair and a nose piercing lugged a canvas suitcase into the center of the room, flipped open the lid, and started removing equipment. The stuff reminded Cassie of a home science kit.

"Almost." The woman smiled as she took out each piece. One looked like a homemade radio, with dials and frequency settings. The other, a simple microphone. She removed a stack of small metal objects, none familiar to Cassie, then set up a tripod and rested a video camera on it.

As the two women worked, the third stood like a statue in front of the oven, palms flat on the stovetop. Maria, a tall woman with gray hair and bellbottoms straight from the '70s, remained still while everyone set up. Viv set a row of candles on the countertop and lit them.

"Really?" Heather looked to Cassie.

She shrugged.

"Excellent. We're ready." Viv offered a smile. "Don't worry. We've done this plenty of times. Just stay back and let us handle it. Things might get intense, but just remember that we're in control. Nothing will harm you. Remain calm and try not to panic."

Heather stood up and stepped closer to Cassie. Jamie took Cassie's hand.

Maria sat in front of the oven, her legs folded, hands resting on her knees.

"Okay. We're recording." Reiko gave a thumbs up.

Viv looked at them. "Last chance. If anyone wants to leave, please do so now."

The girls huddled together.

"Okay, then let's get started." Viv switched off the lights. Only the glow from the candles lit the Home Ec room.

"They can't do their magic with actual lights on?" Heather whispered. "You guys are going to owe me lots of money when this is done."

Reiko stood to one side while Viv stood to the other. They both looked at Maria, whose back was toward the girls.

Slowly, Maria's voice started filling the air. An

unrecognizable chant, a language foreign to all but Maria.

A coldness settled in the air and sent a ripple down Cassie's spin.

"Jennifer? Are you with us?" Maria's voice was low and spellbinding. "If you're here, would you please give us a sign?"

Cassie held her breath and focused on the oven. Heather wrapped her arm around Cassie's forearm, linking them together.

"Jennifer, I feel your presence. Would you please give me a sign so I know you can hear me?"

The oven light turned on.

"Holy fuck balls." Heather jumped and clenched Cassie's bicep.

Reiko shushed them and then focused on Maria.

Cassie bit her lower lip to keep herself quiet.

"Jennifer, we have come to help you find peace. Please, talk to me." Maria's back went rigid.

The oven dinged.

The gray-haired woman kneeled forward, blocking Cassie's view.

"Yes, it's okay. You can talk to me. I'll help you cross over."

Cassie took a step closer, feeling the resistance from Heather and Jamie as they tried to keep her rooted in place. But she couldn't stop herself. She had to see what Maria saw. She untangled herself from her friends. Up behind Maria, she bent down so her face was over the ghost hunter's shoulder.

"You're angry. Yes, I feel it. Someone else has tried to release you from your pain, but you're hanging on. Why?" Maria's voice fogged the glass.

Someone else?

Confusion twisted Cassie's stomach.

Viv and Reiko leaned in tighter.

Jennifer's burned face slammed against the glass.

Maria tumbled backwards. Cassie stumbled away and gasped.

The door opened.

"She can't hurt us." But as the words came out of Viv's mouth, her eyes widened in fear.

"Get back." Jamie tugged at Cassie's hand, but Cassie stayed firm. The whole point of this was to get rid of Jennifer, to be done with this bullshit. And that's what she was going to do. Anger and resolve mixed as she shook off Jamie's hand.

Jennifer crouched on all fours. Twisted tangles of charred flesh hung from one side of her face, her eye bulging from the socket. The overcooked meat scent was heavy—steaks forgotten on the grill, a burger patty slipped into the broiler flames, a hotdog dropped from its campfire spear.

"Do something!" Heather screamed at Viv and Reiko who looked at each other, panic laced tight in their jaws.

"Jennifer, we're here to help." Maria stayed still. "We mean no harm."

A charred stench filled the air as Jennifer slipped one arm out of the oven.

"Shit, shit, shit." Heather ran toward the classroom door, wrapped her hands around the knob. "It's locked! Who locked the fucking door?"

"Viv?" Reiko's breathing increased pace.

Viv ran to the door, pushed aside Heather and tried to open it. "She's right. Okay, everyone relax. Maria, do something."

Maria didn't move as Jennifer stuck another arm out of the oven. She paused, looked around the room, and stopped when her eyes met Cassie's.

Cassie's chest heaved, her teeth clenched. "This ends now."

Something twitched on Jennifer's face. Something sinister and wicked.

She was trying to smile.

Jennifer crawled, slow and deliberate, until her whole body perched on the floor. Hands and feet slapping and crunching against the tile floor. She wore no clothing, but that didn't matter because most of her flesh melted away that fateful night. Only bone peeked through the dead skin, bits of which hung like drapes around her knees.

Maria looked up, her mouth wide open.

"I can't get the door open." Viv's voice strained with desperation.

"Good." Maria jumped to her feet. "We need to contain her."

Jennifer opened her mouth and shrieked. The scream caused everyone to drop. Cassie slammed her hands over her ears until it stopped, then looked up in time to see Jennifer spring through the air like a spider monkey and lunge at Heather.

Heather screeched, but Maria had recovered and was ready. She grabbed one of the metal objects from the floor, a symbol Cassie didn't recognize, and pressed it against Jennifer's back. Jennifer writhed in pain, spine arched and howling.

Viv took one of the other objects and thrust it through Jennifer's skull. Black ooze seeped from the wound, over Viv's hand, running up her arm. Jennifer continued to howl. Maria started to chant while Cassie reached grabbed Heather, pulled her away. Heather sobbed into Cassie's embrace as Jamie watched with wide eyes.

As Jennifer wailed louder, Maria chanted louder. The ooze slid down Jennifer's body, melting Jennifer's corpse with each slow creep until there was nothing left but a pile of bubbling glop on the floor.

No Jennifer.

No body.

Just a mess.

Viv grabbed a bottle of powder from her bag and sprinkled it. It soaked up the glop and left what looked like a pile of wet sand.

Cassie's heart raced as she stared at what was left of the freshman. The only sound came from Heather, who continued to weep.

"Is it over?" Jamie spoke first.

Maria took a small sweep pan and duster from her bag, swept up the wet sand and put it in a glass container, sealing it tight. "She's at peace. We'll make sure this is taken care of."

Reiko stopped recording. She looked around the room. "Wow, that was pretty crazy, am I right? Everyone good?"

"Yeah. I think." Cassie forced herself to give Heather a hug, despite the resentment and anger boiling in her gut.

*This was all her fault and now she can't stomach it.*

Viv collected the various objects and put them in Maria's bag. Maria stood, carefully carrying the jar.

"So, she's gone? We're safe?" Jamie asked.

Maria glanced at her with dark eyes. She looked like she wanted to say something, but Viv stepped up.

"You're safe. But if I were you ladies, I'd keep this to yourselves. Not many people are going to believe it."

"No problem." Cassie gripped Heather. "It's okay. It's all over."

# Chapter Fourteen

## Cassie Adler

"Shit, shit, shit." Jamie white knuckled the steering wheel as she drove out of the school's parking lot. "I can't believe that just happened."

"You and me both." Cassie looked over her shoulder, a part of her expecting to see Jennifer's ghost hurling through the air after them. Instead, she watched the lights of the parking lot grow dimmer. Ahead, Heather's car turned off the main road and headed back to her own house.

"So that's it, I guess."

"You really think so?" Cassie chewed her thumb nail.

"That's what Viv said."

"Yeah, and she seemed to really know her shit."

Jamie chuckled. "Yeah, did you see her face? I thought she was going to hurl at that smell. It reminded me of when we dissected frogs in sixth grade. Remember that gross stench when we cut it open?"

Cassie gripped her stomach as a ripple of nausea

rattled her gut. "Pull over."

"Seriously?"

"Hurry."

Jamie slowed the truck and stopped on the side of the road. Trees lined it and the only light shined from the car's headlights. Cassie tumbled out of the passenger's seat and kneeled on the grass.

"Hey, you okay?" Jamie hurried around the rear end and dropped to her knees. "Just take a deep breath."

"A deep breath?" Cassie chuckled. "You really think that's going to help anything at this point? We just summoned a fucking ghost and then killed it, which means I've basically killed Jennifer twice." She looked into Jamie's eyes. "How did everything get so fucked up? I just wanted them to like me."

"Who? Heather and her sheep?" Jamie sighed. "I know, Cass. I get it."

"No, you really don't. You don't care what people think which only makes you cooler, while I'm working my ass off to fit in and I end up in some crazy ghost story about an oven that captured Jennifer's soul. Oh, and by the way, we still never found her body."

"The body." Jamie sat up. "That's right. I still haven't figured out who watched you that night."

"It doesn't matter." Cassie shook her head. "If Jennifer really is gone, I don't want anything to do with whoever moved her. That person hasn't surfaced so I'm not digging. I just want this all to end."

"I know." Jamie wrapped her arm around Cassie's shoulder and pulled her close. "I really think it's over. We saw her dissolve."

"Yeah, you're right." But the twisting in Cassie's stomach didn't fade.

Jamie sat closer, pulled Cassie tighter. "Hey, you know what will take your mind off this?" She brushed the hair out of Cassie's face. "Homecoming."

Cassie laughed and shook her head. "Oh, man. Can you imagine my biggest problem being what to wear to a school dance?"

"Well, now it is. And you better decide soon. It's coming up soon."

A rustle of leaves shook Cassie's nerves and she pushed away, hurried to her feet. "What was that?"

"Just the wind." Jamie stood, brushing off her knees. "Come on. Let's get out of here."

# Chapter Fifteen

## Cassie Adler

The psych ward wasn't as scary as Cassie imagined. When she called Lauren, Mrs. Fisher answered and explained that Lauren experienced a breakdown. They'd taken her in for observation. Cassie figured the place would be a nightmare. Instead, light green walls decorated with bright artwork, comfy couches for visitors to talk to their loved ones, and a few potted plants lined the periphery. The large windows let the sunlight in, creating warmth and a sense of hope.

Of course, the nightmare might be behind the security doors at the far end of the hall.

Cassie sat on one of the tan couches, smoothed her t-shirt and waited. The security door opened and Lauren stepped through, a nurse walking beside her.

Lauren's long hair hung knotted and frizzy. Her eyes ringed with dark circles and even though she wore her sweatpants and familiar pink sweatshirt, nothing about the teen walking toward Cassie reminded her of the confident girl from only a few weeks ago.

"Here we are." The nurse smiled and ushered Lauren to sit on the couch. "I'll be right over there if you need me." She pointed to a chair just a few feet away and then left the two girls alone.

Cassie cleared her throat. "Are you okay?"

Lauren slumped against the couch. She rubbed her eyes and groaned. "How do you think I'm am?"

"Sorry. Stupid question." Cassie bit the inside of her cheek. "I just wanted to come and give you the good news in person."

Lauren didn't move.

"It's over. She's gone."

Lauren's brows furrowed. "Who? Heather? Did that crazy ghost finally get her?"

"What? No. Why would you think that?"

She shrugged. "It's only a matter of time."

Cassie frowned, pushed the rising fear back. "That's just it. All of this is finally over. We got rid of Jennifer. Sent her back to her ghost realm or wherever the hell she's supposed to end up. We hired these ghost hunters and they performed some sort of ritual. It was crazy, but she's gone."

Lauren huffed and shook her head. "Impossible."

"No, really. I watched it happen, I swear. Jennifer's gone and you can come home, and everything can go back to normal."

"You don't really believe that, do you? That everything can go back to normal?"

Cassie looked down at her lap and shrugged.

"You don't understand." Lauren's voice waivered, tears in her eyes. "It won't be over until I can get it all out, and I can't. I tried, but I can't."

"All what out?"

"The brownie." Tears ran down Lauren's cheeks. "It's still there. Everywhere. I can taste it. It's under my nails, see?" She shoved her hands toward Cassie. "It's coming for me. The monster is still here, just waiting for the right moment. And then, something will come for you and Heather."

"No. Lauren, that's what I'm trying to get you to understand. Whatever happened to us—,"

"So, you've experienced it too?" Lauren's eyes widened.

Cassie tugged at the loose material of her shorts. "No, not the way you did."

"But it was food that came for you, right?" Lauren leaned forward, her elbows resting on her knees.

"Yeah, food." Cassie swallowed the lump in her throat. "A cherry cotton candy tornado."

"Then I'm right." Lauren started to cry, open and louder. "It's not over. *She's* not over. You didn't destroy her because we're still alive."

"Lauren, please." Cassie looked over at the nurse who jumped to her feet. The older woman nodded at group of nurses standing by the reception desk. They stood in anticipation. One took a walkie-talkie out of her pocket and started whispering into it.

"No, no, no, no." Lauren started to hit the side of her head with her closed fist. "You've released her again. You've made it worse."

Cassie jumped to her feet, looked over her shoulder as the double doors opened and a large nurse carrying a syringe came at them.

"Stop, please, everything is okay now. You're

safe." Cassie grabbed Lauren's arms, tried to get her to focus, but Lauren tilted her head back, eyes wild.

"She's coming! She's not done! You only pissed her off even more!"

"Okay, that's enough for the day." The nurse stuck the needle into Jennifer's arm. "Don't worry. We're going to help your friend."

"We're all going to die." Lauren cried as they led her behind the security doors. "She can't stop until every one of us has paid."

Cassie ran out the doors, down the stairs, through the parking lot past a group of smokers in hospital gowns, and to into her car; Lauren's words echoing in her mind the entire drive home.

# Chapter Sixteen

## Lauren Fisher

Lauren lay on the bed, the soothing meds coursing through her veins.

"The monster is coming!" She repeated the words over and over, letting them grow sharp on her tongue. "The monster is coming!"

Sunlight drifted through the barred windows and cast shadows over her simple room. She turned onto her side, curled her knees to her chest, and let the conversation with Cassie repeat through her brain.

Could it be possible? Did Cassie somehow manage to squash Jennifer's hunger for revenge?

Something twisted her gut and cast doubt through her body. Sins can't be forgiven, not without remorse and repentance. At least, that's what she'd learned being dragged to church every Sunday for the past seventeen years.

Remorse weighed down her body, but repentance was long gone. They should have listened to Cassie that night and called the cops.

Why did she always follow Heather? It's not like she and Heather had anything in common outside of soccer. They barely even talked until junior year after Lauren made the team. Before that, she only saw Heather at the cafeteria, sitting with her crew.

Lauren sighed as her eyelids grew heavy. The light shifted. A shadow moved from the corner of the room.

A bolt of fear shot through her. She sat up, stiff despite the drugs swimming in her veins. "Who's there?"

The shadow danced off the wall, twirling along the floor, and narrowing the space between them. Lauren's body shivered with fear as the darkness shaped itself. A torso, arms and legs. Finally, a round head. All cloaked in the black shadow.

"Jennifer?" She croaked and scurried backwards on the bed until meeting the wall. "Please, just leave me alone."

"You know I can't." The blackness molded into a mouth and two shadowy eyes. "You have something of mine."

Jennifer's chest tightened. Her breaths came out short and tight as she trembled.

"You and I have unfinished business." The shadow mouth curled upwards. "You have something that belongs to me and I'd like it back."

"What?" She looked past Jennifer's shadow to the door. Maybe she could make a run for it. Or scream. Would the nurses get here in time? Would Jennifer just kill them too?

"My brownie monster. I want him back. All of him." And as the words came from her mouth, Jennifer whipped her shadow arm through Lauren's body, straight out the other side.

A chill rippled over Lauren, sending her pulse rioting. She gasped as her stomach twisted, a deep pain burning up, rising to her surface. She tasted the ghost of dark, chocolaty chunks, mixed with blood and mucus as she gasped for breath, clutching her gut and praying for this to end.

"It wasn't my fault." Tears clouded Lauren's vision as looked up at Jennifer's shadow. "Heather made us do it."

"Don't worry about her. She'll get what she deserves."

Something twitched beneath the surface of Lauren's skin. She looked down at her arms. Tiny bumps rose to the surface, little bubbles springing to life.

"Oh, God. Please, make it stop." Heat tickled her skin as she gritted her teeth against the pain until she couldn't take it and started scratching. Her nails ripped at the flesh, digging deeper, tearing her skin apart. The tiny bumps popped out of the open wounds.

*What the fuck?*

Horror laced the universe as she furiously tried to comprehend.

It wasn't blood running down her arms, but brownie batter. Rich, dark brownie batter.

She opened her mouth to scream, but chocolate oozed from the back of her throat, choking her words.

"Death by chocolate. Isn't that what you thought while sitting in my brownie monster's gut? Now, you'll really experience it." Jennifer's words, amused and delighted.

Agony erupted in a panicked flash. From somewhere in the distance, she heard a small bell. A timer going off.

Ding.

"It's time." Jennifer smiled.

"No, please." Lauren coughed up the ooze, reached out to Jennifer. But it was too late.

The brownie mix bubbled and Lauren exploded. The walls of Rochelle Hospital dripped with delicious chocolate carnage and the gooey remains of Lauren.

# Chapter Seventeen

## Cassie Adler

Cassie chewed her thumb nail as she sat on her couch watching the Saturday morning news. Her grandma sat on the edge of the recliner, stabbing the volume button on the remote control until it reached max. They'd heard the story reported four times over the past few hours, but their eyes remained glued to the screen.

Lauren Fisher. Murdered in the care of Rochelle Hospital Psych Ward. No suspects at this time. No further details or new updates.

The whole town sat in lockdown. Police encouraged everyone to stay inside, secure their doors and windows, and if they had to leave for any reason, use the buddy system.

The next story flashed on the screen, a picture of Jennifer. She wore a white t-shirt under a bright orange spaghetti strapped sundress that matched her hair. Her eyes shined and a wide smile showed off her high cheekbones.

In capital letters, the word MISSING flashed across the screen.

The image shrank into the top corner of the screen and the squishy face of a reporter filled the extra space. "A missing teenager led police to extend their search to the lumberyard. Nothing found yet, but police urge anyone with information—"

Grandma turned off the television and set the remote on the coffee table. "I'm real sorry about your friends, Cassie."

She didn't reply. She'd barely moved since they'd turned on the news and saw a smiling portrait of Lauren on screen, followed by vague details of her death.

"A lot of shit seems to be going on these days. I want you to promise me you'll stay inside and respect the police's instructions. At least until they catch this lunatic."

*They'll never catch her.*

Obviously, Jennifer murdered Lauren. The cops held back the specific details, but Cassie imagined brownies were involved. And Jennifer did it. She closed her eyes and recounted her visit with Lauren, the ghost hunters before that, the night everything started.

The phone rang.

"Want me to tell her you're busy?" Grandma asked.

Cassie kept her eyes shut. Heather called three times that morning, panicked and whining, scared of the cops, of the ghost, but Cassie didn't want to hear a word.

"You know what, I'll just let it go to the machine. Don't worry about her anymore."

*There's still time to fix this. Jennifer wants you and Heather to pay for what you did, but you're still alive. Get up and fix this before it's too late.*

She looked to her grandmother, whose expression mimicked human empathy for the first time in years.

"Look, Cassie, I know thing's been rough for you."

Cassie rolled her eyes.

"I know I never made it easier, but that don't mean I'm not here for you. Really, that's the one thing I think you could acknowledge. I've always been here. Not like your mom. Certainly, not like your dad, so I think that should be proof enough for you that you've got someone in your life that's stable."

Cassie's face contorted in confusion. "You honestly think simply being a lump on the couch is good enough?"

"Better than any other alternative you got." Her grandma's face narrowed, then she softened her expression. "We don't get to pick our family. You get what you get, and you got me. Believe it or not, I'm doing my best."

Cassie frowned and turned away.

"Now, you need anything? Maybe something to eat? Have you had anything since this dinner last night?"

Cassie ignored the question, stood up, and walked to her room, closing the door behind her. She didn't care if her grandmother suddenly grew a heart and wanted to help. She didn't care about Heather or how scared she was.

"Cassie? Are you sure it's a good idea to be alone right now?" Her grandma called from the living room.

Cassie lay on her bed and pulled her pillow over her head.

"Okay, well. I'll let you rest. Maybe some sleep will do you good."

She'd never been good, never would be. Cassie Adler, the festering boil beneath society's surface, waiting to infect anyone close. Her grandma had a point. You can't pick family, and her family was a giant shit show. One failure after the next, so really, Cassie was just living up to her destiny.

A failure.

A nobody.

No wonder her dad bailed. He possessed the loser gene too, except he tried to escape it, tried to run away, and married someone half his age to start a new family. A part of her wished she knew where he ended up. Maybe if he made it work, she could too. She could leave and start over. Find happiness and a home and a family.

But her gut told her that dear old dad was probably still running, leaving a trail of abandoned children and up-and-coming alcoholic women in his wake.

Or maybe her dad didn't have the loser gene and she inherited it from her mom, a woman who crumbled fast and hard. No wonder her dad bailed. The woman had no grit, no resolve. So yeah, maybe she needed to cut her grandma some slack. The old woman stuck around, took Cassie in, gave her food and shelter.

Or maybe all the Adler women were cursed to never live up to their potentials. Her mom landed in jail over and over, the town drunk who got into fistfights. And her grandma hardened with each new arrest.

And then there was herself. Pathetic Cassie, the youngest of the Adler women trio, so stupid that she believed a group of popular girls would want to hang out with her

She might as well just fall off the face of the Earth. Who would notice?

Lauren and Erin and Heather were never really her friends.

She sighed and flipped on her back, looking up at the peeling paint of her bedroom ceiling.

Really, did any of it actually matter?

She had one person in her life. Jamie. But Jamie would eventually leave, like the others. Either scared off once she heard the news report about Lauren, or some other time in the future when she finally woke up and saw Cassie for the true failure she was.

And then Cassie would be alone.

The way she was always meant to be.

# Chapter Eighteen

## Emily Bower

Emily needed a miracle. Instead, she sat in the teacher's lounge praying to make it through the early morning staff meeting without garnering suspicion. She sucked on a breath mint to cool the morning vodka flavor from her tongue.

"It's been three days since Lauren's death." The principal addressed the staff. "As you know, they have a suspect in custody. Apparently, they think one of the other patients was involved."

Emily shifted in her seat. The news this morning reported a person of interest, a young girl with a love of firecrackers and explosions.

A scapegoat as the community grew restless.

"The cops think we should go back to our normal routines, start trying to heal as a community, and I couldn't agree more, but we have grief counselors available if any of your students think they need to talk."

One of the teachers in the back raised her hand. "What about Homecoming?"

"Still on. The dance is this Saturday in the school gym, and I'd love to have a few more volunteers to chaperone. The more eyes on our students, the better."

Emily caught a quick look from Audrey.

Only a few days to fix everything. But how?

Everything they tried failed and pretending to act normal proved harder than she imagined. First, with Erin's death. Now, she'd do the same with the death of Lauren.

But how much longer could she put up the façade?

And was it worth it?

What if she just came clean? Went to the cops?

No, they'd only say she was crazy and then start tracking down the other coven members, drag them in for questioning. That'd just make everything worse.

It was her mess, her responsibility.

And time to fix it was running out.

The meeting ended and Audrey hurried over. "You look terrible." She kept her voice low.

"I haven't exactly been sleeping much."

They walked out into the hallway and headed toward the Home Ec room. Before they got there, Audrey grabbed Emily's bicep and dragged her into the staff bathroom.

"Hey, what's that for?" Emily rubbed her arm.

Audrey looked into the stalls, made sure they were alone. "You're drunk."

"So?" Emily crossed her arms. "I'm still functioning, aren't I?"

Audrey took a deep breath and looked down at her shoes. "There's something I need to tell you."

Emily's eyebrows rose.

"The High Priestess held a secret meeting last night. I wasn't invited, but I still have a few loyal friends in the coven who told me about it afterwards."

"I'm not going to like this, am I?"

"Just listen." Audrey sighed. "She is planning something against you and me."

A groan slipped through Emily's lips. "Oh, Audrey. I'm so sorry I got you into this mess."

"No, don't. It's okay." She offered a slanted smile that fixed her lips for a split second then slid away. "The High Priestess is dangerous. More than you realize, and she's been growing in power for awhile now. She has access to all the spells from our ancient sisters, and she's been studying them on her own for years. She doesn't just want to hurt you for causing the spell or me for sticking up for you."

Emily's eyes widened. "Cassie."

Audrey nodded. "She's going after everyone, to clean this up, to make the town forget it ever happened."

"Can she do that? Make everyone just forget?"

"From what I was told, she can do just about anything." Audrey's voice dropped. "This isn't what I signed up for. The coven is supposed to be a beautiful connection between sisters, designed in love and to spread love. Not for this. Not for evil and darkness and revenge. We can incite those things, of course, but we're only supposed to resort to those methods if it's absolutely necessary. Like self-defense, you know?"

"I guess that's what she's doing. In a way." Emily frowned. "She's just defending herself against us."

"But it's against the rules." Her voice began to rise. "Never hurt a sister. Never, but she's plotting something awful, something this Saturday at the homecoming dance when she thinks we're too preoccupied to notice. My friends weren't told the exact details, but their scared for me. And I'm scared too."

Resolve settled over Emily. "Then we'll be ready."

For a moment, Audrey's lip waivered, but she steadied her emotions and rolled back her shoulders. "Yes, we'll be ready."

"But there's something we need to do first."

Audrey tilted her head to the side.

Emily squared her shoulders. "We need to warn Cassie."

# Chapter Nineteen

## Cassie Adler

Cassie squinted as the evening sunlight poked through the trees lining her front yard. "I'm really not in the mood for this."

Jamie bent over and touched her toes. "Don't care. You've been moping around, and you need to snap out of it."

"You don't even like running."

"And yet, here I am." She stood tall. "I'm such an amazing friend."

Cassie frowned.

"Besides, didn't you say soccer practice started up again?"

Cassie nodded. Everyone seemed determined for life to move on in Rochelle, including Coach who said the team would start back with regular practices.

"Ready?" Jamie smiled.

"Ugh, fine." Cassie threw her hands in the air. "You win. Let's get this over with."

They started out toward the tree line. Cassie used to explore the woods with her mom long before her family fell apart. A familiar path nestled along the outer edge then wove through a dense bush and into a clearing. She headed in that direction with Jamie close behind. Sweat beaded her forehead, and despite her annoyance, the jog started to loosen Cassie's muscles and calm her nerves. She sped up, the air rushing past her, adrenaline pumping. Jamie huffed and Cassie slowed the pace.

She snickered. "Just remember. This was your idea."

Jamie managed a thumbs up and kept going.

The path lay ahead of them and they were about to enter the woods when a car rolled up.

Cassie slowed as the figure in the passenger's seat waved her hand out of the open window.

"Ms. Bower?" She looked over at the driver's seat and recognized the high school art teacher. "Mrs.

Landry?"

The car pulled to the side and Mrs. Landry shut it off. Ms. Bower got out. She smiled, but it looked tight and forced. "Getting some fresh air?"

Jamie stood beside Cassie, looking from one teacher to the next. "What are you guys doing out here?"

Mrs. Landry stood from the car and looked to Cassie. "We really need to talk to you. Just you. Someplace private."

"Well, that's not creepy at all." Jamie crossed her arms and narrowed her glare. "She's not going any place with the two of you and she sure as hell isn't going someplace without me."

Cassie bit back a snicker as the teachers scowled.

Mrs. Landry shifted on her heels. "We were coming to your house. Your grandmother is welcome to be there, in the home with you, but we just need to speak with you someplace she won't overhear. Would that work?"

"It's about your soccer teammate, Jennifer." Ms. Bower let the words hang in the evening air as Jamie shot Cassie a quick glance. "Please. We're here to help you."

Jamie reached over and held Cassie's hand as she absorbed the information.

"I don't know where she is."

"I know." Ms. Bower's shoulders dropped. "I

burned what was left of her body and buried anything that the fire didn't consume."

Jamie gasped.

"It was you." Heat burned the underside of Cassie's cheeks. "You watched us from the office."

"Yes. No. Well, kinda." Ms. Bower shook her head. "I don't know. It's all very complicated. Please, let's not have this conversation here in the road and not in front of your friend."

"I know everything." Jamie jutted out her chin.

"How do we know you aren't going to hurt us?" Cassie's voice waivered.

"I've always known you were involved, and I haven't called the cops. I don't want anything bad to happen to you, which is why I'm here. I'm not going to hurt you Cassie, but someone else will if you don't listen to what I have to say."

"Who?" Her heart raced.

"Someone much more dangerous than either one of us."

Another car rolled down the road. The driver rubbernecked suspiciously, but didn't stop. Whether Ms. Bower really had useful information or whether she planned to hurt Cassie, one thing remained clear, they couldn't stand on the side of the road forever.

Her mind flashed with the image of the clearing, not that far down the wooded trail entrance from where they stood. It was isolated, which may prove dangerous for her and Jamie, but Cassie figured the teachers wouldn't know the woods the way she did.

"Okay." Cassie let out a deep breath. "We'll talk. Follow me."

———

Cassie sat on the grass, jaw hanging down.

"No. Fucking. Way." Jamie scoffed. "Witches? Impossible."

Ms. Bower told the story twice, each time met with Jamie's curses and Cassie's open mouth expression.

"I think we need to show them." Mrs. Landry placed her hands palm down over the grass. Ms. Bower did the same and started to whisper words Cassie couldn't make out.

She held her breath as tiny daisies sprouted to life, their bright yellow center tilted toward the sun, surrounded by a cluster of white petals.

"How did you do that?"

"We've been trying to tell you." Ms. Bower sighed. "I know it's a lot to understand, but it's very important that you trust me."

Jamie plucked a flower and lifted it to her nose. Her eyes widened as she sniffed. "It's real."

"Of course." Mrs. Landry sat a little taller.

"Okay, so let's say I believe you." Cassie watched Jamie twirl the flower's stem between her thumb and middle finger. "You two are witches and there's a whole secret witch organization that includes a bunch of our teachers."

"Correct." Ms. Bower nodded.

"Your magic trapped Jennifer and now she's using food to kill."

"Yes."

"And now this High Priestess lady wants to kill me and whoever else knows the truth."

"Pretty much."

"Hey, do you think Jennifer killed Erin?" Jamie tucked the flower behind her ear. "I mean, if she killed Lauren and she's after you and Heather, then she must have killed Erin."

"Heather?" Ms. Bower's voice squeaked. "You're not talking about Heather Wilson, are you?"

"She was there too." Cassie nodded. "She and Erin ran into the room after me and Lauren. You probably didn't see her."

"No, I guess not." She frowned.

"It'll be okay." Mrs. Landry rested her hand on Ms. Bower's arm. "We can save everyone."

"Who is the High Priestess?" Jamie asked.

The two teachers looked at each other, then shook their heads in unison.

Jamie huffed. "Oh, come on. You're not going to tell us? After everything?"

"You said you can save us." Cassie focused on

Mrs. Landry. "How?"

"We need to work fast, but we have one final plan."

Ms. Bower nodded. "We're going to end this, but before we do, I need to know one thing."

"What?"

"Do you have your tickets for the homecoming dance?"

# Chapter Twenty

## Cassie Adler

Cassie tied her Sketchers and stood tall. She waited for her grandma to say something from her spot on the couch.

"Don't you want to wear a dress?"

"Not really." Cassie was tired of doing what other people wanted her to do, tired of trying to fit in. She tucked her black blouse into her red dress pants, the ones she'd buried in the bottom of her closet for the past year but never felt bold enough to wear.

"Well, you look fine, I guess. Now hold still so I can get a picture." Her grandma got off the couch and snapped a photo with her disposable camera. A slight smile spread on her lips before quickly returning to a scowl. "You look like…"

Cassie sucked in her breath. *Please, not tonight. Don't bring up mom.*

"You look exactly like yourself."

Cassie released her breath and smiled. "Thanks."

"You be safe, you hear? I want you back by midnight."

"I know." Cassie hurried out of the house and hopped into her car. She wanted to drive with Jamie to the dance, but they decided it'd be best to take two separate vehicles. More getaway opportunities seemed like a good idea, knowing what they were about to face.

As she drove, her stomach tightened. This was it. All or nothing. She revisited the plan over and over. Ms. Bower and Mrs. Landry would be there by now, getting ready. She just had to play her role and stay alive.

Cassie arrived at the school and scanned the crowded parking lot for Jamie's truck. Relief flooded her when she spotted it. Fellow classmates hurried into the school, the girls dressed in sparkles and the guys wearing nice pants and button-down shirts. Music boomed as Cassie stepped into the school, now decorated with streamers and balloons leading toward the gym.

Jamie stood at the entrance decked out in an orange polyester suit complete with ruffled blouse.

Warmth settled in her chest as Cassie approached. "You look incredible. Where in the world did you get that?"

"Thrift store." She smiled and did a twirl. "You like?"

"I love." Cassie grabbed Jamie's hand and pulled her close. The sweet strawberry scent of Jamie's shampoo intoxicated the space between them and for a second, it was just the two of them. "We should probably go inside."

"Probably."

"Ms. Bower and Mrs. Landry need our help."

"Apparently."

"Don't die, okay?"

Jamie laughed, soft and light. "I won't if you won't."

Cassie tucked a loose strand of hair behind Jamie's ear. "Deal."

They stepped into the decorated gym.

A DJ booth sat in the corner, complete with strobe light, and the floor swam with awkward teenagers doing their best to find a beat.

Cassie spotted Ms. Bower and Mrs. Landry by the refreshment table.

"There's Heather and her mom." Jamie pointed to the opposite corner where Coach adjusted Heather's necklace. Coach spotted Cassie, gave a little wave and went back to chaperoning while

126

Heather allowed a sea of girls to flood her. "Wow, she's really handling the death of her friends well."

"This may come as a shock, but I think she likes all the attention. Two dead friends and one missing really upped her status."

"I wonder what she'll do when the attention fades."

Cassie shrugged. "I really don't care."

Jamie snickered. "Well, look at you, all grown up and detached from the mean girl umbilical cord."

"Yeah, yeah." Cassie nodded in Ms. Bower's direction. "Come on. We've got work to do."

# Chapter Twenty-one

## Emily Bower

"You ready for this?" Emily put down her punch.

Audrey gave a quick nod.

Emily locked eyes with Cassie. Luring Jennifer into the open wouldn't be hard, but what would happen after caused her stomach to turn.

One step at a time. They needed help to get rid of Jennifer, and tonight, that's exactly what they would have.

She started to hum the familiar chant, the one Audrey used when they tried to kill Jennifer the first time, the one she now knew by heart. Audrey did the same and moved from the refreshment table into the crowd.

Emily stepped into the sea of teenagers, all of them dancing a similar rhythm to a familiar pop song. She ignored the beat, instead focused on the chant, first humming it as she moved around the outer edge of the crowd, and then softly singing the words as she weaved through.

Audrey did the same, her arms moving with a fluid motion of a ballerina as she twirled to her own song. They crossed paths in the middle, smiled, and kept moving, their words growing louder and their dance becoming more hypnotic.

A few teenagers snickered, but most ignored them.

Emily watched as Cassie and Jamie reached the center of the dance floor. They turned to face each other, holding hands.

Ms. Bates, one of the coven members, grabbed Emily's arm and yanked her toward the edge of the crowd.

"What do you think you're doing? Do you really think this is the way to get back into the High Priestess' good graces?"

But Emily didn't stop chanting. She stomped on the woman's foot. The woman grimaced, dropping her hold. The woman spun on her heel, away. Emily went back to dancing, her chant growing louder. A few teenagers stopped and stared. They pointed and laughed and shook their heads, but the words filled their heads, crept through their minds, and the syllables found their way to the tips of their tongues.

"Stop this at once." Mrs. Reynolds, another coven member, hissed as Emily waltzed by. She ignored the woman.

More heads turned and the teens began to make room on the dance floor, some starting to cheer on their teachers, more starting to hum along to the tune.

A chill raced down Emily's spine as she spun.

*Jennifer's coming.*

She looked for Cassie in the center of the crowd and hurried toward her, chant still singing from her mouth.

Then music stopped. Emily turned. The High Priestess was at the DJ table, eyes burning with anger and jaw grinding. "I'd like to see Ms. Bower and Mrs. Landry in the hallway, now."

Emily whispered in Cassie's ear as she passed, "Stay away from that woman. She's the High Priestess," and then kept dancing.

# Chapter Twenty-two

## Cassie Adler

Cassie shook her head as Ms. Bower floated past.

*She's the High Priestess.*

Impossible.

It's one thing to learn her teachers practiced witchcraft, but she refused to accept that her soccer coach was their leader.

"Coach is the High Priestess." The words jumbled in her mouth.

"That explains Heather." Jamie snickered. "Takes one to make one."

"But, that can't be right. Coach is so sweet and patient and..." She gasped for a coherent thought. "She'd never hurt someone."

"Or she's just really good at pretending to be someone she's not." Jamie frowned. "Think about it. Would you ever have pegged any teacher in this place for a witch? Or what about Ms. Bower? Think of all she's done in the past month and she still got up and came to work and acted normal."

"Yeah, I guess."

"Even you and I are pretty good at keeping secrets."

"I suppose." Cassie shook all over. "Sorry. It's just hard to wrap my head around."

"I know, but nothing has changed. We need to stay focused."

"Right. Focused."

"Mom!" Heather screeched from the front of the gym. "Turn back on the music!"

130

The lights flickered.

Cassie swallowed hard and let go of Jamie's hands. "I'll see you when it's over, okay?"

Jamie gave a nod, her eyes filled with worry mixed with resolve. Cassie turned and ran. She pushed her way from the crowd, from her innocent peers, grabbed Heather's arm on the way out of the gym and dragged her to the hallway.

"What the hell? Why'd you do that?"

"Hurry." The urgency in her voice got Heather's feet moving, and despite being in high heels, she managed to keep up as Cassie tugged her away from the crowded gym. No need for the entire school to fall victim to Jennifer's wrath.

Somewhere, down the hall, a sound rang out.

Ding.

"Stop." Cassie skidded to a halt. "Did you hear that?"

"No. Hear what?" Heather twisted away from Cassie's grip. "What's going on? You know, I called you. A dozen times. What, you're too good to talk to me all of a sudden?"

"Shut up." Cassie's heart raced as she ran down the hall where the ding came from. Her pulse quickened as terror balled in her chest. "Fuck."

Jennifer levitated in at the far end of the hallway. Her body limp and sagging, as if an invisible noose held her to the ceiling. Except, she wasn't dead. Her head tilted to the side and sadistic smile spread over her face.

Heather screamed and faltered backwards. She regained her balance and took off running.

"Wait!" Cassie turned and bolted after her.

They turned the corner and found themselves running down the by freshman rooms. Heather whimpered as she fumbled with the doors, only to find each of them locked. She raced to the women's bathroom, pushed, and gasped with relief when it opened. Cassie followed, locking it behind them.

"We can't hide forever." Cassie grabbed Heather's shoulders and gave a hard shake. "Stop crying. I need you to focus, okay? We have to get back to the Home Ec room."

Tears streamed down Heather's flushed cheeks. "Why won't she just leave us alone?"

"Because we killed her!"

A sound came from one of the nearby bathroom stall. A gurgle that bounced off the walls.

Cassie let go of Heather and took a step back. She moved towards the first stall. The sound got louder. Her heart raced and a bead of sweat dripped down her spine. With a hard push, she swung open the door and sucked in a breath.

A red liquid bubbled in the toilet. A fruity scent swirled in the air.

"What is it?" Heather's voice held a desperation

that caused Cassie's nerves to jump.

"I think it's..." She took a step a little closer. The liquid bubbled higher and spilled over the rim. "Toilet punch?"

And just as she said it, the fruity liquid erupted from the toilet in one grand fountain, shooting to the ceiling and back down, showering Cassie with tangy nectar and orange slices. She gasped and stepped back, slipping on the floor and crashing to the ground. The other toilets erupted, one at a time, until they rained fruit punch from the heavens, drenching both girls in sweet syrup.

Heather screamed and dropped to the floor, covering her head with her arms as if that would do any good.

"Don't just sit there, run!" Cassie fumbled to her feet as Heather unfroze and darted toward the bathroom door. Cassie fumbled with the deadbolt, finding everything slick.

"Come on!" Heather shouted.

The liquid burped and bubbled as it rain over them, flooding to past their ankles.

"Hurry!" Heather hit Cassie's shoulder.

The locked relented and the door swung. Their feet slipped and skidded on the waxed floor, but they managed to stay upright as a wave of punch busted out of the bathroom and chased them down the hallway.

The wave's crest grew as Cassie chanced a quick look behind her. A second later, her entire body swam within the liquid, pummeling her with tidal force. She flipped, letting her body grow slack against the current. Heather whipped past, a look of terror written on her face. Cassie's lungs burned as the punch slammed her from one side of the hallway to the next, crashing her into the lockers without mercy. An image appeared within the wave.

Jennifer.

Shit.

Cassie kicked her feet and flailed her arms, trying to swim up, hoping to find an air pocket.

She didn't.

A hand wrapped around her ankle and tugged, dragging her back down. Cassie stared directly into Jennifer's face, the fruit punch swirling around them. She tangled her hand in Cassie's hair and pulled her close.

*This is it. I'm going to die.*

She struggled, but Jennifer pressed her lips to Cassie's.

Cassie gasped, but not in real time. Her body remained in the punch wave, lips tight against Jennifer's, but her mind reeled with images of flames licking her skin and melting her clothing. Pain seared her nerves and sizzled down her body leaving no hair untouched. The unrelenting heat penetrated every pore as she screamed in agony.

*Please, make it end. Just kill me.*

Smoke filled her sinus and burned the back of her mouth as she tilted her head back and roared. Her hands balled into fists and she slammed them against the glass, begging for help that wouldn't come.

Then, Cassie was back in the punch. Except, it started to drain. She had no idea where it was going and she didn't care.

Jennifer was gone. At least for now.

Cassie coughed and gasped. A jackhammer throbbed behind her eyes and when she reached up and touched her forehead, blood coated her already sticky fingers. Heather lay on the ground beside her, spitting up punch and wheezing, and orange rind nestled into her ruined hair.

"I saw it all, from her point-of-view." Cassie sucked in a deep breath. "She showed me."

Heather closed her eyes and rested her head against the wall. "It was just a stupid prank. Do we really deserve all this?"

But before Cassie could answer, the locker doors shot off their hinges, propelled by gusts of fruit punch.

One slammed into Cassie's face with a crack. Sharp pain radiated from her nose and she winced as blood flowed, the metallic taste slipping between her parted lips. She dropped low, flattening herself against the floor as the doors continued to fly. Binders and books catapulted, slamming into her back.

She clenched her jaws and covered her head, tried to ignore the pain.

Heather cried. "Please, stop! We'll do anything you want, just make it stop!"

Silence.

The doors dropped to the floor, the flying pens and folders landed on the ground, and the punch rolled down the hall and out of sight.

"Do you think she's done?" Heather looked to Cassie.

Cassie pushed herself up and looked around at the debris. Only one locker remained closed. It creaked open as a ripple of fear slid beneath her flesh.

A moldy sandwich flipped out of the locker and landed in the center of the hall, blocking the path back to the Home Ec room. It was as much blue and green as it was white and brown.

Heather stood, her entire body trembling. "What's with the PB&J?"

The two slices of bread pursed together, as if they were lips, and whistled. All around the floor, bits of discarded food, long forgotten by their owners, moved toward the bread.

"Cassie?" Heather stepped back.

A blackened banana climbed on top of a pile of chewed bubble gum. A lollipop with a single dark hair stuck to it bounced onto the pile. Half-eaten granola bars, a melted Hershey Kiss, potato chip crumbs all joined forces. The bubble gum linked them together, wrapping around and around, growing taller and wider as a lone grape rolled over. The leftovers stood almost the height of the ceiling and close to the width of the hall, its body formed like a linebacker.

The moldy sandwich sat on top and started whistling *We Are the Champions*.

Cassie's breaths quickened. "I think I preferred the cotton candy tornado."

"The what?" Heather's eyes widened.

The leftovers stomped and the ground shook.

"You know, I'm really getting tired of all of this." Cassie straightened her back and planted her heels. "Either kill me or get the fuck out of the way."

It dropped to all fours and galloped full speed.

Cassie gritted her teeth and charged. She counted on the creature going low and when it did as she hoped, she went high, leaping off the ground and landing on the other side in a roll. It turned and snarled, the banana serving as lips.

"It's just like soccer." Cassie called out to Heather, who stood cowering in a corner.

"Dismantle the offense. Literally."

That seemed to wake up Heather. She ran forward and kicked its calf, a chunk of moldy blueberry muffin flew, hitting the wall with a goopy navy-colored splatter.

"I think it'll work. Nothing's filling the gap."

Cassie jumped on its back. "Keep attacking!"

Heather kicked at its apple kneecaps. Seeds clattered down the hall before sticking to the punch leftovers. The creature groaned and swiped out its arm, shoving Heather into the lockers.

"Shit." The gum lashed out, snake-like, and tangled around Cassie's arms and legs.

"Cassie?" Ms. Bower's voice echoed through the hall.

"A little help would be great!"

Cassie balled up her fist and punched into the creature's back.

Heather managed to make it to her feet as Ms. Bower and Mrs. Landry joined forces attacking the beast, tearing at the food. The moldy sandwich stopped whistling and started snarling. Its arms grabbed Ms. Bower first, pulling her off her feet and slamming her to the ground. It turned its focus and spit a wad of gum at Mrs. Landry's face. The gooey bits webbed over her eyes as she fell backwards.

"Cassie, do something!" Heather kicked loose a granola bar, sending oats and over-dry raisins in every direction.

"Working on it." Cassie wiggled her fingers until they touched a cold, slimy ball of a variety of shades. She gritted her teeth and tugged. The moldy sandwich let out a yowl as Cassie tore out its heart.

A giant sticky jawbreaker candy.

She dropped to the floor as the monster crumbled. It fell, piece by piece,' until the floor looked like the remains of a wild food fight.

Heather brushed crumbs out of her hair. "Now what?"

Cassie forced herself to her feet. She wiped a blob of mold-green yogurt from her cheek. "Now, we go back to where it started."

# Chapter Twenty-three

## Cassie Adler

Cassie stood in front of the Home Ec oven. Heather and Mrs. Landry sat in chairs, collecting their breath while Ms. Bower started to chant.

"So, the chant will kill her?" Heather asked.

"As long as Jamie got enough people to do it." Mrs. Landry nodded. "Jennifer's too strong and not interested in leaving. We need a massive amount of force to overcome her. The trance we started will do just that. The more who participate, the stronger it will become and the greater chance we have to defeat her."

"You're wasting your time."

Everyone turned. Coach stood in the threshold, her jaw tight, fists balled at her sides.

Cassie's heart dropped. So it was true. Coach really was the High Priestess.

"Mom, oh thank God." Heather jumped to her feet and hurried to her mother. "You won't believe what just happened."

"I bet I can guess." Coach opened her arms and let Heather rush into the embrace. "Oh, sweetie. You should have come to me the minute all of this started."

"I know. I'm sorry."

Coach rubbed Heather's shoulders and smiled. "Stand beside me, okay?"

Heather did as she was told, a small smile of satisfaction spread on her lips.

Coach glared at Ms. Bower, who stopped chanting. "That spell might weaken her enough to send her away, if you managed to get enough people singing it, but it won't be permanent." She walked into the room and pointed at Mrs. Landry. "I'm so disappointed in you. I hope everything you've put your sisters through has been worth it."

"It was." Mrs. Landry rolled back her shoulders.

"You don't deserve to be High Priestess, you never did. You're nothing more than spoiled, entitled asshole and soon everyone will know the truth."

Coach's mouth twitched but she remained still.

"Mom?" Heather looked from Ms. Bower to her mother. "Aren't you going to protect me now that you know the truth? I really need your help. Cast one of your protection spells or get rid of this curse on me. Please."

"Wait, what did you just ask for? Are you serious right now? You *knew* your mom was a witch?" Cassie hissed the words. "All this time, you knew your mom ran some underground witch club?"

"Of course, I knew." Heather snapped back. "Unlike you, my mom actually loves me and doesn't keep secrets."

Heat raged through Cassie's core, but she bottled it. For now.

"Mom, please."

"No, you have to face Jennifer." Coach's voice softened and for a second, Cassie saw the woman who ran practices and gave inspiring pep talks. "The girl's soul is trapped by a need for revenge, but even an emotion as dark as hatred can be overcome. Prove you're sorry. Don't just say it. Atone. It's the only way to break the spell."

"Great fucking words of wisdom, Yoda." Cassie's nostrils flared. "We've all been sorry since it

141

happened, and she's killing us one-by-one."

"I said atone. Don't just rattle off empty apologies. There is no other spell breaker."

Ms. Bower sneered. "So, you knew I couldn't break the spell? You knew it and yet you put me and Audrey in danger?"

Coach sighed. "To teach you a lesson about consequences and humility."

"I can't do this anymore." Heather's voice cracked with panic. "She's going to kill me. I need to leave before it's too late." She pushed her mom aside and ran out the door. Coach turned on her heel and hurried after.

"That's just great." Ms. Bower shook her head.

Cassie focused on the oven, her heart thumping. Nothing came out. No cotton candy fog. No crazy sinister dessert hell bent on revenge. No ghost.

"Maybe the chant actually worked and what Coach said was a lie." Cassie looked to Mrs. Landry and then Ms. Bower.

"Maybe." Ms. Bower's voice filled with uncertainty.

Mrs. Landry sighed. "But what if she was telling the truth?"

"Then, what is Jennifer waiting for?" Ms. Bower asked, looking at the oven.

"An offering," Mrs. Landry whispered, her eyes shining with the truth.

"A trade." Ms. Bower's voice dropped. "Oh, God. It can't be. She wants to exchange her trapped soul for another's."

Cassie let the idea settle. Of course. Saying she was sorry and actually showing it were two different things.

"No, not a trade." Cassie shook her head as the weight of what was unfolding crushed on her shoulders. "A truce."

Ms. Bower's eyes moistened with tears. "You don't have to do this." But even as the words came out, Cassie knew they were a lie.

She closed her eyes and took a deep breath. Her dreams of leaving Rochelle would never come true, but as her mind whirled with possibilities—college, a career, a family—they settled on a single image.

Jamie.

Cassie smiled.

She picked Jamie and Jamie picked her. They were family. Always had been. And she'd gotten three years of warmth and happiness and love.

It'd have to be enough.

Cassie opened her eyes, peace resting on her shoulders.

Mrs. Landry's bottom lip quivered. She gave Cassie a tight hug and then stepped back.

"Cassie, I..." Ms. Bower trembled as tears dripped down her cheeks. "I'm sorry."

"Me too."

She took a deep breath and kneeled down. The darkness inside the oven called to her as she steadied her trembling hands and crawled forward. The space barely fit her. She tucked her knees to her chest and twisted her neck to the side so she could see out of the glass.

The door closed and locked with a small click.

Her chest rose and fell quickly as the oven walls confined her. Panic bubbled to her throat, but she swallowed down the acid and looked out at Ms. Bower whose flat palms pressed against the glass.

Cassie's mind raced.

Would this be enough to save Heather too?

Anger crept to the edges at the thought of Heather walking away from all of this with nothing more than a toilet fruit punch stained homecoming dress. But she didn't want anger to be her last emotion.

A cry pierced through the glass door and a second later, Jamie shoved Ms. Bower aside and slammed her fists against the class.

"No! Don't do this!"

Tears welled up in Cassie's eyes. "It's okay. I promise."

Jamie's eyebrows pinched together as she clutched the oven's handle and tugged. She looked over her shoulder at the two teachers. "Help me, don't just sit there!"

"Honey, this is the only way." Ms. Bower tried to pull Jamie away, but she shoved the teacher back.

"No, this can't be how it ends." Jamie searched the room as Cassie watched.

"Jamie, stop."

But she didn't listen. She grabbed a chair and threw it at the glass.

Cassie winced at the echo. "Please, you have to accept this."

"How can you say that to me?" Jamie dropped to the floor and pressed her forehead against the glass.

Cassie moved her hand and pressed her fingertips against the door. "Jamie, I love—"

The coil above Cassie's head turned red. Cassie sucked in a breath as the temperature crept from cool to warm. Small beads of sweat lined her lip as she tucked her head as low as possible to keep, but frizzy tendrils of her hair sizzled on the warm coils. Her pulse quickened as Jamie kept pounding on the glass, her screams doing nothing to stop the rising heat.

"Jennifer." Cassie whispered as moisture dampened her blouse. "Let's trade places."

And then she appeared, sitting right next to Cassie. Except it wasn't the horrific image that haunted everyone for weeks. The Jennifer sitting next to Cassie shined. Her auburn hair lay past her shoulders and her round face glowed with peace.

Jennifer's green eyes searched Cassie's face. They ignored the screaming from the other side of the door, the pounding of fists and the wailing. Cassie's fear steadied. She sat relaxed and ready to serve her penance.

The temperature continued to rise. Cassie's lungs worked overtime to filter the stuffy thick air. She struggled to breathe as Jennifer leaned forward. Their lips almost touched, and a wave of dread washed over Cassie at the thought of another kiss with Death.

But Jennifer paused.

She pursed her lips, but didn't move any closer. Instead, she let out a long deep breath of cold air. It chilled the small space and formed small specks of ice that dropped and simmered on the coils. The temperature lowered quickly as the coils darkened to charcoal grey.

Hope rooted in Cassie. A relaxed smile settled over Jennifer's lips. Jamie stopped banging on the glass.

The outline of Jennifer blurred and began to fade. She looked at Cassie, still smiling, still glowing and relaxed.

"Even good people make mistakes."

Cassie's mouth opened but no response came out. She stared in awe as Jennifer faded away.

The door popped open.

"Cassie!" Jamie grabbed Cassie's arms and pulled her out. "You're alive."

She let Jamie squeeze as tears flowed.

"I thought Jennifer got to you."

"No, she's at peace now." Cassie pulled away, but kept her arms around Jamie. "I thought I'd never see you again."

"It's over?"

Cassie nodded, certainty settling over her tired body. She looked at Ms. Bower and Mrs. Landry. "But what about the coven and Coach?"

Ms. Bower shrugged. "I don't know, but I think I need a break from the kitchen for a bit."

Jamie wiped her soggy cheeks. "What about you and me? What's next for us?"

Cassie smiled. "Your mom wanted us to have an adventure. Maybe we should go check out this dance everyone is talking about."

# Epilogue

## Heather Wilson

Heather loved college, despite missing out on a soccer scholarship. Her mom managed to grease the wheels of the admission board and Heather got a walk-on spot at her dream school's soccer team. She never asked questions when opportunities fell into her lap. Whatever means her mom used to help worked just fine. One day, Heather figured she'd do the same for her own kids.

Part of a coven or not, the woman still used her power.

Once a witch, always a witch.

She slipped the tiny white sundress over her head and admired her curves in the full-length mirror. The west coast sun did wonders for her skin, and she glowed a light olive complexion that complimented her newly dyed auburn hair.

Not even a scar remained from a year ago, and the lunatic ghost. She flashed a smile and licked off the red lipstick that smeared the front of her teeth, determined to push back the rising memories of her past.

Once deer hunters found Jennifer's teeth unearthed in the woods, it wasn't long before bits of her clothing and the remains of her bones were discovered. The town went into another panic. No one was ever accused or convicted, so Heather was in the clear, but she didn't like being around the drama.

Now, she had a fresh start.

Away from Cassie—who still played on the Varsity team for her senior year.

Away from her mom—who was trying to start a

rival coven. Ugh, the drama of it all.

"Hurry up. Sarah said to meet them down in the parking lot. She'll pick us up in five minutes." Heather's roommate Adrianna rushed out the door.

Tonight, Heather planned to get wasted with her sorority sisters, like a normal college girl. She puckered her lips in her room's mirror and fluffed her hair.

"I'm coming." Heather stuck a condom in her purse, just in case. As she walked toward the door, she spotted Adrianna's stash of homemade churros, still fresh from her mom's weekend visit.

Her stomach growled. She'd been on a protein only diet lately, but one churro wouldn't kill her.

Heather grabbed it, the sweet scent of cinnamon watering her mouth, she took a bite.

"Mmm." Heather moaned and smiled. She shoved down the rest of the treat, licked her fingers and turned toward the door.

She took one step and another, but slowed and then stopped

A sour taste bloomed behind her teeth as her throat tightened. Something slithered past her tongue and when she opened her mouth, a tiny baby churro slid down her chin and dropped to the floor.

Panic laced Heather's chest. She looked back at the plate of churros and whimpered.

They wiggled and slipped off the porcelain, down

the desk, and onto the floor, little cinnamon sugar worms falling into formation. The one that fell from her mouth began climbing her bare ankle. Her heart raced as she squealed. She swatted at it, but it dug sugary teeth into her skin. Heather gasped at the site of a single dribble of blood running away from the fresh wound. She grabbed the door handle and pulled it open.

Jennifer stood on the opposite side of the door, burnt as the day she died.

"Fuck."

# Acknowledgements

A big thank you to Unnerving and Eddie Generous for putting out the submission call and making this book a reality.

Chris, thank you for always supporting my wild dreams, for allowing me to brainstorm death scenes over the dinner table, and offering endless encouragement. Without you, this book wouldn't exist.

Charlie, I love you so much. You're an incredible potato, and you inspire me daily. Thanks for telling me you can be anything if you only believe.

To the entire amazing Scifi&Scary crew, thank you for being my horror family and accepting my weirdness. You inspire me.

Thank you to Justin Fulkerson and K.A. Tutin who diligently critiqued my work. You two helped mold it from a pile of scribbles into an actual story.

To my family (Marc, Lynn, Marilyn, Mike, Emily, Ashley, Ryan, Lori, Sue, Eddie, Matt, Jessica and David) and my dear encouraging friends (Angela, Jennifer), thank you for cheering me on!

And finally, thank you readers. You rock my socks off!

# REWIND OR DIE

Midnight Exhibit Vol. 1

Infested - Carol Gore

Benny Rose: The Cannibal King - Hailey Piper - Jan. 23

Cirque Berserk - Jessica Guess - Feb. 20

Hairspray and Switchblades - V. Castro - Feb. 20

Sole Survivor - Zachary Ashford - Mar. 26

Food Fright - Nico Bell - Mar. 26

Hell's Bells - Lisa Quigley - May 28

The Kelping - Jan Stinchcomb - May 28

Trampled Crown - Kirby Kellogg - Jun. 25

Dead and Breakfast - Gary Buller - Jun. 25

Blood Lake Monster - Renee Miller - Jul. 23

The Catcatcher - Kevin Lewis - Jul. 23

All You Need is Love and a Strong Electric Current -
Mackenzie Kiera - Aug. 27

Tales From the Meat Wagon - Eddie Generous - Aug. 27

Hooker - M. Lopes da Silva - Oct. 29

Offstage Offerings - Priya Sridhar - Oct. 29

Dead Eyes - EV Knight - Nov. 26

Dancing on the Edge of a Blade - Todd Rigney - Dec. 12

Midnight Exhibit Vol. 2 - Dec. 12

www.UNNERVINGMAGAZINE.com